Soul Mates

By
John R. Little

JournalStone
San Francisco

JOURNALSTONE
YOUR LINK TO ARTISTIC TALENT

This is a work of fiction. All of the characters, names, incidents,
organizations, and dialogue in this novel are either the products of the
author's imagination or are used fictitiously.

JournalStone books may be ordered through booksellers or by contacting:

JournalStone
www.journalstone.com

ISBN: 978-1-942712-41-1   (sc)
ISBN: 978-1-942712-42-8   (ebook)

Library of Congress Control Number: 2015942297

Printed in the United States of America
JournalStone rev. date: August 14, 2015

Cover Art and Design: M. Wayne Miller
Cover Photograph © Shutterstock.com

Edited by: Dr. Michael R. Collings

There was only one possible choice of dedication for this book:
To my soul mate, my amazing dream girl,

Fatima Monteiro.

Acknowledgements

Thanks to my pre-readers, who constantly notice things I can't see myself: Tod Clark, Dave Solow, Shelley Milligan, and Sydney Leigh. Special gratitude to Dr. Michael Collings, who edited this novel and helped make it much better than it was before he got out his red pencil.

Endorsements

Prolific fantasy and horror author Little (*DarkNet*) revels in the dark recesses of the mind and the pull of the forbidden in this tangled novel. Savannah and Alannah are identical twins who move to Seattle to escape their parents' tragic past. Alannah soon finds love with the magician Jeremiah, who has his own demons to wrestle with. Meanwhile, both sisters are plagued by the hauntings of an unknown boy. Little writes with vivacity and a sharp eye for detail, recalling Hitchcock in his use of twists and turns and the unexpected; his characters are layered and intriguing. The book has a decidedly nonlinear narrative, which heightens suspense, but some of the places where Little weaves the separate strands together feel rushed. Readers will find the sense of immediacy refreshing and enjoy the complex, horrific story. - Publishers Weekly *(Aug.)*

"*Soul Mates* is an exquisitely haunting novel of deeply etched characters and bone-chilling terror. It's impossible not to fall under its magic spell. A superb book from one of the genre's finest talents." - Brian Pinkerton, author of *Rough Cuts* and *Anatomy of Evil*

"There are two words you don't often, if ever, hear when describing a "horror" writers' work – Wordsmith & Elegant. But, that's exactly what kept running through my mind as I read John R. Little's *Soul Mates*. If you've never read any of Little's work, you're really missing out. Not only does he weave a wonderfully horrific tale, but commands his prose like so few in the writing community can do on a consistent basis. I'm dead serious about that and *Soul Mates* is no exception. I've read everything Little writes and you should too. You're most certainly in for tasty treat with this one!" – Ty Schwamberger, author of *The Fields, Deep Dark Woods* & *Escaping Lucidity*

"John R. Little takes readers on a journey into the dark corridors of the psychic in his novel, *Soul Mates*. Prepare for a wild ride of suspense, mystery, romance, and horror. This is a book that stays with you long after you finish reading. Highly recommended!" – Kenneth W. Harmon, author of *The Amazing Mr. Howard*.

Soul Mates

"It's so quiet," Luke said.

Charlie nodded at the ghost of Finn.

I miss you, babe.

He knew she'd reply, *I miss you, too,* if she was able.

The canoe pulled out farther into the lake. The water near the campground was still, as it formed a harbor for small boats to tie up. Now, away from land, the lake water rushed quickly from Charlie's right to his left. He had no trouble controlling the boat, though. The time he'd invested in canoeing with Finn was paying off as he navigated into the rougher water and smiled as Luke's head bobbed. He grabbed the sides of the canoe and laughed. Charlie knew that sensation and he smiled.

"Are you sure this is safe, Dad?" Luke looked back, and Charlie realized his son was getting a little too nervous.

"It's okay. I'll turn around and head back to the calmer waters."

He maneuvered the oar down and used it to shift them to the left.

That's when he heard the cries. At first they were indistinct, barely audible. He glanced at Luke, but everything was fine there. Then he looked back to shore and his world collapsed.

What the hell?

On shore, he could see Mary Lamot. She was near her cabin, just at the edge of visibility. She was screaming.

She had Dylan in her arms, holding the three-year-old as high as she could.

It wasn't doing any good.

At Mary's feet were two dogs. Charlie recognized them instantly—Jack Russell terriers owned by a twenty-something camping at the far end of the park. The dogs barked incessantly whenever Charlie and the boys happened to walk near them, and more than once he'd wondered why anyone in his right mind would want to own animals that just seemed mean.

The owner had just shrugged and smiled, as if the growling dogs straining to get loose from their leashes were normal, everyday pets.

Now they were loose and jumping onto Mary in a frenzy. Even from this distance, Charlie could see that her face was dripping with blood.

"Oh God . . ."

She was losing the fight. With the scent of blood being spilled, the dogs were becoming even more violent.

In her upstretched arms, Dylan looked like a rag doll. The dogs were biting and clawing him non-stop.

Charlie froze. His son was being ripped to shreds in front of him, and he was 500 feet away, unable to do a damned thing.

I'll never get there in time.

But he had to try. Panic spread through him, and in a decision he would regret for the rest of his life, for some reflex reason, he stood up, forgetting where he was.

The canoe capsized, and Charlie was under water. Although he'd forced Luke to wear a life jacket, he hadn't worn one himself. It took him a moment to realize what had happened. It may have been a hot summer day, but the lake water was as frigid as it had been in March. His body fought the cold, and he splashed frenetically to try to find the surface.

When he did, he was staring toward the shore, and once again he saw Dylan's body being attacked by the half-crazed dogs.

Mary was unable to hold the boy any longer, and they both fell to the ground. Charlie couldn't see them anymore, but he heard the screams and the dogs barking.

No, not Dylan. Don't take him from me, God.

"Dad!"

Shit.

He swiveled in the water but couldn't see Luke.

"Dad!" The sound was quieter now, but Charlie could finally make out Luke being swept away by the rushing current. He disappeared from view.

Once again Charlie froze. He needed to go after Luke, but he needed to rescue Dylan from the dogs.

Luke had a life jacket.

With little conscious thought, he swam as fast as he could toward shore.

* * *

Three months later, Luke's body was found twenty miles downstream. By the time the original search party had started to look for him, he had been lost for almost an hour, and they never had a chance. The only people available to search were the handful renting cabins. The guy who owned the Jack Russells wasn't around. Later, he'd swear he'd had them tied up but they somehow got loose.

Dylan lived, but he lost one eye and had fifty stitches snaking over his body. It took him six months to recover physically, and he never did recover emotionally. He never spoke a word the rest of his life, and his remaining eye always seemed haunted.

Charlie in turn was haunted by the ghost of Finn and—now—of Luke.

They followed Charlie wherever he went.

Part 1

Introducing!

"For centuries, magicians have intuitively taken advantage of the inner workings of our brains."

—Neil deGrasse Tyson

Chapter 1
2008

Savannah Clark was sixteen years old when she left home. She didn't think of it that way herself, because to her it felt much more like her home left her.

What was left?

She didn't take much with her: her diary, of course, because that was her. Sometimes the diary felt more like *her* than her real body felt. She tossed the few clothes she liked into a travel bag, along with her toiletries, and, really, that was about it. A hairbrush. A Coke she stole from the fridge and one small stuffie: a fist-sized gray-and -white kitten she'd had since she was a baby.

While Savannah was packing, Alannah was doing the same thing, but Savannah wasn't thinking of her sister. She didn't have to. They were identical twins, and they always marched to the same tune. They barely had to talk to each other to know what the other was thinking, and they always took the same approach to life, no matter how different they were.

Savannah paused after filling the bag with her meagre belongings and listened. She thought she heard footsteps from the living room below.

Dad.

That would be the last thing she needed.

But it was also impossible. He was behind bars where he belonged.

She cocked her head to one side without thinking, like a lonely puppy, but she didn't hear any further noises.

Just paranoid after last night, she told herself.

Even so, her body froze in place and she was breathing heavily. She wanted to ignore the imaginary sound but her body wouldn't let her.

"There's nobody there," she whispered. "Not even Alannah."

She blinked and licked her lips. Finally, she took a deep breath.

"This is ridiculous."

She picked up the bag and walked to the door of her bedroom, pausing to take one last glance before leaving. She wouldn't really miss the poster of One Direction hanging on the wall or the pink housecoat hanging on the bedpost. Even though Mom had given it to her three Christmases earlier, she'd never liked it.

Mom.

She did then remember one other thing she wanted. She went to the bottom drawer of her dresser and found an old photo of her mother and father.

She ripped it in half and left her father's image in the drawer. Savannah stared into her mom's eyes as she carried the picture to the bag and slipped it inside.

Then she really did leave, never looking back.

There was nobody in the main floor of the house, as she logically knew, but she felt relief anyhow.

Soon, the twins left their childhood home for the last time.

* * *

Savannah's mother was Marianne Clark.

Marianne had a bit of an obsession with the deep South, having watched *Gone With the Wind* dozens of times when she was a young teen. She imagined living in Atlanta or some other faraway southern city, dreamed of living in steaming summer heat and cool winters, wanted romance and adventure to be a part of her life the way it had been for Scarlett in the movie.

She grew into a pretty teenager, hardly noticeable among hundreds of other pretty teen girls in her hometown. She would sometimes stare in the mirror and wonder how she could become the girl every guy wanted.

Her hair was long and blonde, but it could never hold any curls. Her eyes were gray, not green or bright blue. Her figure was nice but ordinary.

Then she found the secret she desired and found she could have any man she wanted.

On her seventeenth birthday, she snuck into a neighborhood bar called The Wrong Number. The lighting was always dark, and as long as she carried herself with confidence and acted like she belonged there, nobody ever asked her for ID.

It was the night she wanted to lose her virginity. She decided she'd waited long enough. In her mind, a southern belle should be worldly and experienced, and it was time to get some of that.

She ordered a glass of the house white wine and sipped it at the bar as she looked around. The guys close to her were all her father's age, nothing interesting there. She ignored them.

Rock music blared through a hidden speaker system. Nobody was dancing.

Part of her wanted to sneak out the door, but once she started down a path, she didn't abandon it, no matter how foolish it started to look.

She finished the wine and ordered another. In the dim light, Marianne wasn't sure she'd find anyone, but then she walked to the far side of the room and saw him.

Tall, dark-haired, muscular, dressed in jeans and muscle shirt, a white cowboy hat sitting on the table with his beer.

He was alone, seemingly daydreaming. She sat down at the same table with him.

"Well, hello there," he said. He smiled and looked confused.

Then she did her thing.

She smiled. Not just an ordinary smile that you'd give a passing stranger. No, Marianne knew by now exactly how to get noticed. She opened her mouth when she smiled and widened her eyes. She knew that when she did that, no man could miss her. Then she moved her chair an inch closer.

It was all to say: *You're special and I am dying to fuck you right now.*

Never failed.

He leaned over and returned her smile, but his was tentative.

"What's your name?" she asked.

"Brian Clark. You?"

"Marianne."

She kept her smile focused on him; he couldn't keep his eyes off her. She licked her top lip.

"I've been looking for you," she added.

He didn't know how to reply, but after a few drinks together, they left the bar behind them. He was twenty-four and had an apartment nearby. Marianne's wish to lose her virginity came true.

Her first sexual encounter also brought her an unexpected surprise: she soon discovered she was pregnant.

Oh, crap, she thought.

Her parents refused to help her, but she didn't really care. She used her smile on Brian Clark, who didn't want to lose fucking privileges since he rarely got any elsewhere. He asked her to move in with him, and they eventually married.

None of that stopped Marianne from perfecting her flirting. After all, Brian was just one guy. She needed more. She kept the smile and wide eyes going whenever she wanted to have a bit of fun. She liked having men notice her, and whenever Brian wasn't nearby, she'd use her skills to attract whoever was handy.

Sometimes it didn't go beyond harmless puppy-dog stares from the guys she focused on. She liked knowing they wanted to fuck her, and it gave her the power to deny them.

Once in a while, though, things went further. She'd find a way to lead them off to an alleyway or somewhere else private, and she'd make out with them for as long as she could. Having men fawn over her was the best feeling ever, and as the years went on, Brian became unimportant except as a source of family income.

About every second or third year, she would sleep with one of the men she conquered, and that kept her satisfied for a while, until the urge came upon her again.

Over the years, she became more careless, and she sometimes thought Brian suspected her of cheating, but she also cared less and less.

Brian had hit the limit of his tolerance, however. He was growing insanely jealous of all the times he suspected his wife of cheating. His friends had sometimes wondered if she'd been stepping out on him, and that was just not something he could allow to continue.

Finally, when Savannah and Alannah were sixteen, Brian decided he would no longer ignore it. Something had to happen.

That night, Marianne left to go to do some unspecified chores, and Brian followed her to a motel on the edge of town. He saw her greeted by a stranger, and he saw *that* smile on her face as she went inside.

Angered, he took his shotgun with him. He no longer cared what happened. The curtains were drawn so he couldn't see inside, and he couldn't hear anything, either.

I know what you're doing, you miserable bitch.

He ran at the door and crashed into it with his shoulder. The cheap door sprung open, and he saw his wife lying in bed with the stranger.

Just for a split second, she smiled, as if she had gained some type of fabulous satisfaction. The guy with her was pissing himself.

Brian didn't hesitate. Without a thought, he killed them both.

The police arrived fifteen minutes later and found him sitting on the only chair in the room. The shotgun was lying on the bed, below the bodies. He admitted killing them and said he had no regrets.

Two hours later, somebody at the police station phoned Savannah. That was when she decided she was going to leave her home and never return.

The twins never knew what motivated their father to murder their mom. In their minds, it was irrelevant.

Chapter 2
2005

Three years earlier.

When Alannah Clark was thirteen years old and looked at herself in the mirror, she saw her twin sister, Savannah. The image looking back at her had long blonde hair, a thin body, long legs, and a killer smile. They both had learned from their mother how to use that smile to their advantage.

None of Alannah's friends had ever said it must be weird to live with somebody who looked exactly like her, but if they ever had, she would have replied, "It must be weird for you *not* to."

Sometimes she would try to imagine life without her twin, but she just couldn't. It wasn't just that they were born looking the same; they *thought* the same, too. They knew exactly what was going on with each other, even without sneaking a peek at each other's diaries. (And, although both denied they did that, they both knew it was just one more secret they shared.)

That's where the similarities ended, though. They shared appearances and they shared understanding and they shared thoughts, but their personalities couldn't have been more different.

Alannah spent her summers wandering through the ghost town that was her local library. Nobody seemed to read books anymore, and she was often the only one in the quiet building. She liked that. The quiet comforted her, like a quilt she could snuggle into in front of a warm fireplace.

Books enlightened her. Peace enveloped her in golden pleasure. Dealing with actual human beings, on the other hand, was a stressful chore. She was a gentle little soul who always felt inadequate, unless she happened to be pretending to be Savannah. *Then* she could somehow find the courage to fit in.

That rarely happened, though. The twins enjoyed fooling others, but only rarely.

One warm June day, she was just finishing skimming a new section of the stacks. She flipped through a couple dozen books on biogenetics, not really knowing what the heck it even was, and she finally decided to head back to the fiction section instead. That's when she bumped into the boy.

He was as startled as she was. He had his nose in a book and hadn't been paying any more attention than she. Her bum smacked into his.

Alannah stepped back with instant fear but almost immediately relaxed when she saw the same expression on his face. He was about her age or maybe a year older, dark brown hair neatly trimmed, wearing a white polo shirt with an emblem of some fancy clothing company that she didn't recognize.

"S-s-sorry," he said. At first it sounded like he was whispering, but she nodded and smiled.

"I was just—" She pointed in the general direction of fiction.

"Oh, sure."

He pressed himself to the stack and let her pass.

"Hey," he said. "Are you Savannah?"

"No, that's my sister. Do you know her?"

He shrugged. "I think you guys live near me. Over on Partridge Circle, right?"

The Circle was exactly that. It was a road shaped like a ring that only had one connecting road joining it to the rest of the Aynsville. Most of the houses on the Circle backed onto forest, and the neighborhood kids spent much of their summers building forts and exploring the wilds.

"What number?" she asked.

"At 102."

"We live at 63. Opposite side, I guess."

They were both quiet for a few seconds.

"Maybe I should go home," said Alannah.

"I can walk you. I'm Tom Gillespie."

"Alannah Clark."

* * *

Over the next two weeks, Alannah and Tom became good friends. They liked to read and spend time walking through the forest together. Neither really cared much for groups, so they were happy to have an excuse to avoid them by hanging out together.

Alannah wrote about Tom in her diary. Otherwise, Savannah might never have found out about him.

* * *

But Alannah *did* write about him, and Savannah *did* find out.

At first, Savannah didn't care. After all, she and her sister wrote nearly every detail of their lives in their diaries, like some weird competition to see who could write the biggest mass of boring, everyday details.

Whenever Savannah was alone in their shared bedroom, she went to the bottom drawer and lifted Alannah's diary from underneath the gaudy Christmas sweater that Aunt Alice gave her two winters earlier. These days, there were often entries about Tom. Tom and Alannah walked to the woods or they went to the library yet again or they found their way to the store and shared a Coke. It was nothing special, which is one reason Savannah zeroed in on it. How fun would it be to treat the "nothing special" boy to a surprise?

She put the diary back and checked herself in the mirror, which she knew was stupid. Of course she looked exactly like her sister.

She brushed her long blonde hair and practiced smiling at herself.

The sun was shining brightly, and she was wearing a short-sleeved, light-green top with a matching skirt when she walked out and headed toward 102 Partridge Circle. At first she didn't see Tom, but she stood on the sidewalk and looked up to see him wave at her from a top-floor window.

Within a half minute, he was bounding out the front door.

"Hey," he said. "What's up?"

"Just wanted to see you," she said. "I thought we could go for a walk."

"Sure."

Tom smiled. His voice was soft and kind, and Savannah could see right away why her sister liked him.

She took the lead and walked behind his house. There was no fence separating the property from the forest. One day there might be a whole new neighborhood built on the rough land, but for now, everyone on the Circle enjoyed the tranquility.

Not too far from the Circle, there was a small pond. Savannah led Tom there and as they got closer, she reached for his hand. She smiled to herself after seeing the shocked look on his face when she did that.

This is going to be fun.

They got to the pond and looked across the water. In the distance, two wild ducks were swimming. Tiny circles spread out from mosquitos landing on the water.

"It's nice here," she whispered, trying to sound meek and nervous, like her sister might.

Tom didn't reply, just nodded.

She turned to face him.

"Have you ever kissed a girl?"

His eyes grew wide.

She wanted to laugh at his fear, but instead she just smiled. When he didn't answer, she moved toward him and pulled his head close.

Savannah had never kissed a boy, either, but that didn't bother her in the slightest. In her mind, she was now Alannah.

She guided Tom's face to hers. His lips were dry. She kissed him and then licked his lips. He kissed her back.

He really liked it.

She put her arms around his neck, trying to remember what she'd seen in movies and television. She started to get a bit scared but then remembered the fun that she was sure would happen the next time Tom was alone with Alannah.

Open your mouth, she told herself. *That's the way they always do it in the movies.*

But she didn't have the courage to go that far.

Fortunately, Tom had watched movies, too, and she felt his lips part. His tongue moved awkwardly between her lips, and she thought it was about the most gross thing she'd ever felt.

She reached out with her own tongue, and she almost started to laugh when they touched.

They kissed for several minutes and he moved his arms behind her back, pulling her to him.

Oh, my.

She felt his erection pressing against her, and it took all her willpower to not just slap him and run away. She'd heard about boners but had never felt one.

Curious in spite of her fear, she reached to the front of his shorts and pressed her hand against his cock. He made a whimpering sound but didn't stop kissing her.

Can I?

She rubbed his pants and then decided to go for it. She undid the button at the top of his zipper and reached her hand inside.

When she touched him, he moaned and kissed her harder. She wondered if he wanted to touch her in her private places, too, but he kept still, as if he were a statue. She felt his cock and squeezed his balls lightly.

Suddenly, he groaned and bent over a bit. Her hand was sticky, and she pulled it out and broke the kiss.

"Ohmygod," he said. "I'm so sorry. I didn't mean to—"

She rubbed her hand on the grass and smiled at him.

"Don't worry. I liked it."

That was the grossest thing ever.

He buttoned his shorts.

"I should maybe clean myself," he said.

She nodded.

They walked out of the forest, not talking, not touching, each wearing a smile. His was real. Hers was, too, but not for the same reason.

"Next time, you be sure to touch me, too," she whispered when they got to his house. "It'll be even better."

His smile grew wide.

"I want that," he said.

"Me, too."

* * *

Two days later, Savannah dug out Alannah's diary and flipped to the most recent entry, which had been written the night before.

* * *

Tom was at the library today, but I only saw him for a few minutes. He had this weird grin on his face, but whatever.

I really wanted to just be alone and browse books, so I told him that. He said he just wanted a minute, so I sighed and sat with him.

He gave me a locket.

A locket? Why? I told him it's not my birthday or anything, but he just gave me that goofy grin again. The locket had a letter A engraved on it.

The A is for Alannah? I didn't really ask, more like told him, but it turns out I was wrong. He said it stands for Angel. He said I'm like an angel to him.

The whole thing was getting just a little weird, but I do kind of like it. It's gold and the A has this funny style, like old-fashioned writing or something. I told him thanks, and I patted his arm and he giggled like a girl. I really just wanted to get away so I put the locket in my pocket and went to find the astronomy section. I wanted to find out more about comets, 'cause there's been something about a comet in the news.

* * *

Savannah put the diary back and found the locket, also buried in the same drawer.

"A for Angel, huh?"

She felt a tug of disappointment. Nobody had ever given her a locket.

"If they had, it would be S . . . not for Savannah, but for Shit-Disturber," she whispered.

She put it back and closed the drawer.

After another couple of days passed, she checked the diary again. There was nothing written in it. Another week passed and still no new entry.

Of course, Savannah could never ask Alannah what was up.

The diary stayed empty for two weeks. And Savannah never saw the locket again. It had been swept out the door along with the memory of Tom.

She smiled when Alannah started writing in her diary again, never again mentioning Tom.

Later that summer, Savannah did buy herself a locket with the letter S. She liked it.

Chapter 3
2008

Alannah Clark had always enjoyed living in upstate New York, but when her father murdered her mother, she agreed with Savannah that a change would be good.

Not just good—mandatory. She never wanted to see him again, and besides, there were too many memories of her mother haunting her there.

The twins left their home that morning with no end in sight. Neither had ever left the state before. Alannah was scared. If it'd been completely up to her, she probably would have procrastinated long enough to eventually decide to stick it out.

Savannah had no such hesitation. Once she had an idea in her mind, it was time to execute it. Alannah always, *always* did what her twin did. There was no need to ponder about right and wrong. She just followed her sister. Period. She liked that. It wasn't her nature to be a leader, and that was just fine with her.

They started by walking south. Both carried backpacks stuffed with a few clothes and even fewer keepsakes from their former home. Between them they had about $200. They had just passed their sixteenth birthdays.

Savannah wasn't worried in the slightest.

Alannah wasn't worried either, but only because she knew her sister would make things work out. She walked on the side of the road leading out of town. They hadn't talked about a specific strategy, but I-90 was only about ten miles south and it seemed like the best place to catch a ride.

A ride to where? wondered Alannah.

The morning sun beat down on them. Alannah wore dark glasses and a light blue cap that matched her T-shirt. She wore a slightly darker color of shorts and her well-worn sneakers. She was used to walking, and she loved the quiet of nature, so the trip south was actually enjoyable.

At times, she felt guilty about leaving the place where her mother was buried, but that never lasted long. Mom would have understood that they needed to get away from their father. Staying in the town where he was in jail for murdering her wasn't an option. What if he got out on parole? Even if he stayed in jail, would he expect them to visit him? The thought of that made her shake with anger.

I'll never see you again.

She knew what they needed: a fresh start. And they were on their way.

As they walked, a couple of cars passed, but they didn't try to hitch a ride. Getting to the 90 was the easy part, and they did it within three hours, even taking a rest break about halfway.

Alannah knew that they'd have little trouble catching a ride on the interstate. She just took off her sunglasses and cap and wore a big smile whenever a car drove by. It was something she'd learned from Savannah.

Sure enough, they had a ride within ten minutes, from a college boy who was almost as nervous as Alannah was. He only took them the first fifty miles of their journey, but they never had to wait long for a new ride.

At the end of the day, they found themselves in the southern Minnesota. Their smiles had gotten them that far and also encouraged the drivers treat them to lunch at McDonald's and dinner at Arby's.

The cooler night air made Alannah happy. Most of the cars they'd been in hadn't been air conditioned.

They stayed at a cheap motel. Alannah didn't watch when Savannah took over and went into the office. She didn't come back out for an hour and she carried a key to one of the rooms.

That night, Alannah slept peacefully. She dreamed about when she had been a little girl and her mom had squatted on the floor to play with her Barbie alongside her. It was a nice dream, and when she woke the following morning, she kept her eyes closed and soaked in the memory. She wasn't completely sure how much of the memory was real and how much was wishful thinking, but it warmed her heart.

"I miss you, Mom," she whispered.

A phrase flashed through her mind: *A agua esta fria.*

She lurched to sit up.

What?

The words meant nothing to her. She didn't even know what language they were in. Or maybe it was just made up nonsense.

A agua esta fria.

"Spanish?" she asked nobody.

The phrase stuck to her and she wondered if it was from her dream.

There was a knock at the door. She jumped and shook the odd words from her thoughts as she pulled back the curtain from the window. She recognized him; it was the guy from the front desk.

She opened the door.

"Is everything okay?" she asked.

He smiled. "Just finished my shift like I told you earlier and wondered . . ."

"Wondered what?"

"If you wanted some company. That was awfully nice when you checked in. It was worth the free night's stay, that's for sure."

Oh, God, Savannah. Really?

Alannah tried to smile but she felt trapped.

"No, I'm sorry, I need to—I need to do something."

She pushed the door shut and leaned against it. The door was flimsy and she could hear him mutter something, but she ignored it.

Savannah wasn't in the room. Alannah felt a stab of loneliness, but she felt happier when she heard the clerk walking away.

Alannah showered, enjoying the hot water splashing down her face. It was one of life's little pleasures.

After drying herself and her hair, she dressed in a second pair of shorts that she'd brought for the trip and a white cotton top. It was going to be another hot day.

Finally, she did what she'd planned ever since waking. Since she was alone in the room, she picked up Savannah's journal and flipped to the last page.

* * *

Savannah — July 15. It was a freakishly hot day and sad in many ways, but you know me. I don't dwell on the sad things. I prefer the limitless possibilities of the future.

Where will that future take us? I don't know. I know that right now, we're traveling to somewhere that will be exciting and interesting.

I'm writing this at 4:42 in the morning. The sun is trying to rise and I just got back from a walk. Nothing beats walking in mid-night during summer.

There's a lake not far from here. Glen (the clerk who bartered a free room for us) told me about it and I walked over there tonight. It was serene and I walked out until the water was up to my knees.

And I could have sworn I heard a little kid whispering something. *A agua esta fria.*

I don't know what it means or even if I've spelled it right. Have a feeling the "agua" means water, which made sense, but the rest means nothing. I'm pretty sure it's Spanish.

After I heard the phrase, I looked around but didn't see anything. Maybe it was just the wind. Maybe it was my imagination. Who knows? LOL!

I should get some sleep, but I'm too hyped up. Maybe I'll go for another walk soon. We'll see.

* * *

Alannah stared at the pages. There was that phrase again.

"How the hell is that possible?"

She was sure she'd dreamed that exact same phrase. Confused, she thought about Googling the unusual words but they didn't have a computer. They probably had one in the office she could finagle using, but she didn't want to run into that clerk again.

The twins had the closest relationship anybody was capable of. She knew that. But dreaming a phrase that showed up in Savannah's diary was just weird.

She picked up the journal and flipped to the next page. They'd agreed that to reduce the amount of belongings they had to carry while hitch-hiking, they'd share a journal.

* * *

Alannah—July 16. I'm ready to hit the road again. I'm not as excited about this trip as Savannah, but I agree we needed a change.

I'll miss our home, but we'll soon have a new one.

* * *

Alannah felt like she should write more, but she couldn't think of any more words. A tear rolled down her cheek as she closed the book.

Chapter 4
1984

Jeremiah Moore was ten years old when he decided he wanted to be a magician.

Before that day, he'd hem and haw when anybody asked what he wanted to be when he grew up. The best answers he could come up with were a cop or a teacher. Maybe a monkey trainer at the zoo. But he always seemed to squirm inside when he said those answers.

There was a guy who lived down the street named Paul something and he was a cop, but he mostly complained about his job, like it was totally boring. He seemed to want to find ways to avoid going to work by pretending he was sick. Jeremiah knew he was faking, because he was always well enough to want to toss a football around with him and the other kids on the street. Somehow being a cop didn't seem as exciting as it did on television.

As for a teacher? Well, he had Mrs. Simmons as his fifth-grade teacher and she was okay, but she seemed bored, too. She liked to assign desk work and then she'd just stare into space, like she was imagining a holiday in Mexico or maybe just a day away from the class.

Monkey trainer? Who knew?

Teacher? Cop?

Once upon a time, when he could barely understand the concept of a job, he'd wanted to be a bus driver. His mom never stopped telling people about that, like it was the funniest joke ever. He hated her saying that. Didn't *somebody* have to be bus drivers?

That looked pretty boring these days, too, driving the same routes over and over again.

At times he wondered if it'd be fun to be an actor. Or maybe a comedian. Something in front of an audience sounded right up his alley. He wasn't shy and loved to be the center of attention.

So, when grownups asked what he wanted to be, he'd politely answer, but never with anything close to what he really wanted . . . because he just didn't know.

He once watched a TV show about a drifter, a guy who moved around the country and helped people everywhere he went. If he was honest (and he never was about this topic), that was the way he'd like to live. Spend his life traveling around the United States, seeing everything, meeting lots of people who would be thrilled when he helped them out of a jam, and make sure everyone was always happy.

Somehow, even at ten, Jeremiah sensed that wasn't actually a very likely career path.

His world-view changed on May 24, 1984. He had just had his birthday two days earlier, so he'd easily remember exact the date forever.

"Mom, do we have to watch this?"

He was sitting at the kitchen table with his mother. Dad was working late again, and it was just the two of them sharing some leftover ham and scalloped potatoes. Mom had cooked a big meal the day before, because that was just what she always did on Sundays, and Mondays were relegated to being leftover day.

No wonder Dad works late a lot on Mondays, he thought.

He picked at the food, wishing they could at least watch something interesting on TV like *Fraggle Rock, The Transformers,* or *Fat Albert,* but Mom never budged. It was time for reruns of *The Phil Donahue Show.*

Mom loved Mr. Donahue's talk show. She never called him Phil. Jeremiah couldn't understand it. Well, maybe he could. He was funny enough, but his guests were mostly old, so he didn't really care about them.

"Quiet, sweetie."

He picked at some potatoes and sipped his milk. He wondered what would happen if he just dumped the milk on the table. Would that take priority or would Mr. Donahue?

"My next guest is amazing! He's performing at the Selton Theater in Times Square. Please welcome the amazing Michael Cooper!"

The studio audience went crazy, presumably knowing who this guy was. Jeremiah had no clue.

He walked on stage, and magic happened. Literally.

It wasn't just the actual magic tricks he performed, it was the effect it had on Jeremiah. He had never really watched a stage-magician perform. Cooper started with some fast tricks, one after the other: making a top hat appear out of nothing; conjuring at least a dozen white doves out of the hat, then the birds flew around the stage and disappeared one after the other back into the hat, which promptly vanished.

"Whoa . . ."

His mom glanced at him and smiled.

The magician's assistant rolled in a contraption that looked like a box on wheels. Cooper waved a wand around it (*where did that come from?*) to show that there wasn't anything connected to the box. His assistant climbed inside, and he did some hocus-pocus to make the box levitate.

He twirled his wand and the box rotated in time with his movements. It spun faster and faster, until Jeremiah figured the girl inside must be about ready to puke her guts out.

Suddenly Cooper stopped, and the box crashed to the floor, splintering into a hundred pieces.

The audience gasped.

There was no sign of the girl.

Jeremiah's mouth hung open. He was riveted, along with the audience, not to mention his mom.

That was the exact moment he knew what he wanted to be when he grew up.

* * *

The Toy and Game Emporium was almost a mile from Jeremiah's home. He lived in a suburb of Cleveland, a city that seemed to stretch forever. There were three toy stores that Jeremiah knew about, but the Emporium was the only one he knew how to walk to. He also knew he shouldn't do it, but he figured he could go there and get back in an hour. Mom was watching her soaps on TV and wouldn't notice he was gone.

He hoped.

He ran much of the way, but every few minutes he'd stop and walk. He didn't really know why he did that, but he was nervous and figured if anyone saw him running, they might think something was wrong. Jeremiah didn't want anybody to ask what he was doing. Even though there was no school today and lots of kids were out on the streets because it was a nice warm day, they weren't running alone down the main street.

The Emporium had a grander name than it deserved. It was a narrow store that stretched back quite a long ways, crowded with shelving that only allowed two tight passages.

There was a teenager sitting at the front behind a desk. He was reading a tattered paperback book with an almost-naked girl on the cover. He barely noticed when Jeremiah entered.

Jeremiah had been in the store before, but never by himself. His mom had taken him a few times to buy toys with money he'd received for birthdays or Christmas from relatives who'd had no idea what a ten-year-old boy might like.

The front of the store displayed the most popular toys: Barbie dolls and accessories, Yo-Yos, Legos, and other stuff that he never cared for. As he moved down the aisle, he found stacks of toys he'd never heard of and then a big section of board games.

He was beginning to think he would be out of luck until he noticed a section to his right containing magic tricks.

Jeremiah stared at the items. He didn't know where to start. There were big packages and small ones, all promising *Amazing! Stupendous! Real! Magic!*

He grabbed one and looked at it: Dr. Magico's Deluxe Magic Kit #1.

Dr. Magico's name appeared on a lot of the toys.

"Oh, wow . . ."

There were about a dozen magic tricks included in the box, and he felt a rush of excitement, imagining learning every one of them and putting on a magic show for his friends.

He knew that this was the beginning of his new life.

Then he saw the price tag. $59.99.

Jeremiah's heart sunk. He only had about two dollars in his pocket.

Unlike some of his friends, Jeremiah didn't receive an allowance from his parents. They thought it was stupid to pay their kids for surviving another week. Occasionally they'd offer him a dollar if he'd take all the garbage out or help clean up the garage or run to the corner store to pick up some milk. That wasn't very often, though.

He wasn't sure how many of his friends received an allowance, but he thought most of them did. It was something nobody talked about. *He* never talked about it because he didn't want to have to admit he didn't get any money. He figured his friends who did have an allowance didn't talk about it, either, because they didn't want to feel awkward saying they got money to somebody who didn't. So, it was one of those secrets that none of the kids in the neighborhood talked about.

$59.99.

He put the kit back.

"Must be something . . ."

He poked around, paying more attention to the prices than what the tricks were, but there was nothing he could afford.

"Shit."

He glanced around, worried that somebody might have heard him swear, but there was nobody there. The guy at the front of the store was out of sight, nose buried in his titty book.

Jeremiah wanted everything on the shelves. Everything. The big magic kits (numbered 1 through 4), the decks of cards, the wands, the magic candles, the coins, the little balls, the top hats, the handkerchiefs . . . everything. He needed it all for his new life.

Unfortunately, he could afford not a single kit. The cheapest toy was $7.99: a set of magic balls that would disappear.

"So cool . . ."

Jeremiah picked up the kit. Dr. Magico's Disappearing Balls.

It was a plastic pouch, but he couldn't see inside. All he knew was what was printed on the outside of the package:

> Your audience won't believe their eyes. Right
> in front of them, these magic balls will disappear
> into thin air. Only you control them. Only you
> have the magic touch to make them reappear.

Before Jeremiah knew what he was doing, the little plastic pouch was in his pocket. It bulged a bit, but he didn't think it really showed.

"I need it," he whispered.

As he walked to the front of the store, he thought of the probable phone call to his mother from the clerk, saying he'd caught her son stealing. He'd be in such crap. He slowed his walk, and almost gave up, wanting to put the magic trick back on the shelf.

"Help you?"

He almost jumped at the clerk's voice. The guy was still sitting behind the old wooden desk, and he wasn't really paying attention. Jeremiah figured he just wanted the kid to leave.

"No, I'm good." Somehow his voice didn't crack, and he marched out the door.

When he got home, his mother was still glued to the television watching *Days of Our Lives*. She didn't notice when Jeremiah ran up the stairs to his bedroom and clicked the door closed.

He didn't have any scissors, so he had to rip the bag apart. At first he wasn't sure he could do it, because the plastic was quite rigid, but he managed eventually. He poured the contents out on his bed.

Three small, hard, rubber balls popped out, each about the size of a ping-pong ball, and a little piece of paper containing the instructions.

Magic balls.

His mouth hung open in amazement as he picked one up. It felt like a normal rubber ball, but smaller. He examined it but didn't see anything special.

Finally he read the instructions and realized something he hadn't known about magic: it was a trick.

The balls weren't magic after all. There were three sections to the instructions. First, he would have to learn to juggle the balls. Second, he'd have to learn how to hide one of the balls in the palm of his hand and make it stick there. The instructions said he should practice with a quarter and then once he knew how to palm a coin, start practicing with the ball. Third, he had to combine the two steps so that when he juggled, he would make one of the balls "disappear" by palming it.

The instructions covered one small piece of paper. There were a few diagrams to show how to juggle and palm, but not much more.

"Eight bucks for this?"

Surely the other magic kits were real magic. This must just be some weird thing to get people interested.

But most of the others were also manufactured by Dr. Magico.

He looked at the instructions again and tried to follow the steps to juggle the balls. He dropped them all.

The balls lay immobile on his bed, and he was very close to throwing them into the garbage.

Instead, he picked them up. He thought about the instructions and realized it didn't matter that the balls weren't actually magic, as long as it looked like they were.

He studied the pictures and tried again. Again they fell.

Two weeks later, he was able to juggle all three balls for minutes at a time without dropping them.

Palming took longer. The coin he practiced with never wanted to stick properly, but three weeks later, real magic happened, and he could hide a coin easily. Another week, and he was able to hide one of the little balls.

Putting the steps together took another few days to perfect, but he was soon at the point where he could juggle the three little balls and then one of them would just disappear . . . just like magic.

At first, he thought he couldn't show his mom or dad, because they'd want to know where he got the money to buy the balls. But then he realized the balls were probably only worth a few cents each. He could say a friend gave them to him.

Jeremiah's first magic show was on August 12. He made his mother and father sit in the living room while he shoved a towel down the back of his neck for a cape and came into the room with a flourish, welcoming them to the First! Ever! Jeremiah Moore! Magic! Show!

They smiled.

Then he started to juggle the little rubber balls, and they were startled to realize he could do that.

When the first ball disappeared, their jaws dropped.

He never told them how he did it.

The following week, he walked to the Toy and Game Emporium and stole a magic wand.

Chapter 5
1987

It took three years for Jeremiah to shoplift $1,000 worth of merchandise from the toy store. He knew exactly how much it was because he kept meticulous track of everything so that he could pay the money back one day. He never lifted more than one thing per month, worrying that the sleepy clerk would wonder why he was there so often. As it was, the guy never seemed to notice any damned thing.

Twice he bought tiny items, cheaper toys from other parts of the store, hoping that nobody would connect him if they ever noticed that the supply of magic tricks was slowly dwindling.

Every time Jeremiah took something, he felt a twinge of guilt, but he didn't quite know what to do about it. He had no other way to obtain the tricks, and he knew he absolutely had to have them. He needed them as much as he needed food. Sometimes more.

The magic tricks were stored under his bed, where his mom wouldn't find them. He wondered sometimes if that would actually matter, because every once in a while, she'd walk into his bedroom and find him practicing a new routine, but she never asked where he got the illusions. It was like she assumed they were old toys from Christmases past or some other appropriate venue.

He shared his bedroom with his brother, Scott. Scott was three years younger, ten to Jeremiah's thirteen, the age when Jeremiah had decided to become a magician, his whole life spreading forward from that one episode of *The Phil Donahue Show*. So far, Scott had no such calling. He'd just play with his Legos and action figures.

Today, he was playing with a 500-piece jigsaw puzzle of a map of the United States, with each state a different color than the ones touching it.

"You'll never finish that," said Jeremiah.

Scott shrugged and then said, "I will if I want to."

"But you won't want to. You never do."

Scott reached over and turned up the radio. It was already loud but this was his way of telling his brother to shut up because he wasn't listening to him.

Whitney Houston belted out her new song, "I Wanna Dance with Somebody." Jeremiah hated that song and wanted to hammer the radio to rat shit to shut it up.

Their bedroom was on the second floor of a small house in the seamier part of Cleveland. Even at thirteen, Jeremiah knew that nobody would live in this neighborhood if they could afford to live somewhere else. Anywhere else.

"Do you have to do that right there?"

Scott had the box of puzzle pieces beside him, blocking the doorway. He'd fished out as many of the edges as he could find, and they were scattered all around.

"Hello? Are you going to answer me?"

Jeremiah stared at his little brother. Sometimes the brat just drove him batshit crazy.

Scott glanced up and smiled, then stared back down and tried to shove two blue pieces together. They didn't fit.

Jeremiah felt a familiar feeling. He clenched his teeth and wanted to hit something. There were times when he had no control over his temper, and Scott's dismissive glance had brought him to one of those points, anger flooding him like a tsunami. He pushed his brother aside and grabbed the box of puzzle pieces, took the whole mess out of their bedroom, and threw them down the stairs. Most landed with a clump at the bottom, but the middle and lower steps were sprinkled with puzzle pieces, as if they were confetti.

That wasn't enough.

The anger still welled up inside Jeremiah and demanded action.

Scott's one and only serious hobby was his collection of model cars. He had built models of a half-dozen classic cars, all lined up on a bookshelf on his side of the room.

He worked meticulously on every one, gluing the tiny parts together and painting each car before attaching the appropriate decals. A car could take him a month to build, sometimes more.

Jeremiah grabbed the cars in turn and threw them as hard as he could to the bottom of the stairs. When each landed, it splintered into pieces, the model glue not nearly strong enough to hold together after being smashed onto the linoleum at the bottom.

It was only when the last car (a red '66 Ford Mustang that had taken Scott a full three months to painstakingly assemble) fell to pieces that the sudden onset of anger dissipated, and Jeremiah stared down at the carnage he had created.

"Oh, no . . ."

Scott hadn't said a word, his mouth hanging open, tears falling down his cheeks.

"I'm sorry," Jeremiah said. "I—I'm so sorry."

The radio was blasting away to the next song, Los Lobos singing "La Bamba." Scott crawled onto his bed and buried his head into his pillow.

Jeremiah felt like shit. He wanted to hide, and that's what he did. He knew nothing he could say would make Scott feel better, but he had to try. He said, "I'm sorry," again, and then left. He had no other words.

Jeremiah was careful not to step on any of the pieces on his way down the steps. Then he ran out the front door and kept running until, panting, he stopped sometime later. He looked around and didn't know where he was or what route he'd taken to get there. All he had thought about was the look of bitter betrayal on his little brother's face.

* * *

It wasn't the first time Jeremiah Moore had lost his temper in a split second. It had often happened while playing baseball with friends, almost always resulting in him coming home with a black eye, a puffy cheek, a loose tooth, or some other surface damage. He wasn't the biggest or strongest kid in the neighborhood, but his temper seemed to think he was. Almost all the other kids he played with had no trouble cleaning his clock when he came up to them, fists pounding.

It had been early afternoon when he'd destroyed his brother's models. Part of him wanted to stay away from home forever, rather than face his parents (and more, face Scott). It was getting dark, though, and he did finally angle his way back.

When he walked into the house, the area at the bottom of the stairs was empty, all the little plastic automobile parts gone, along with all the puzzle pieces.

His father came out and stared at him.

"That was quite a mess," he said. His voice didn't sound angry . . . more frustrated. He'd seen the results of Jeremiah's temper tantrums before.

"I know." He didn't know what else to say.

"Come here."

Jeremiah sat beside his father on the lower steps. He didn't know what to expect, but it sure wasn't what his dad finally said.

"I had the same problem when I was a teenager. No control at all. I know the incredible rush that takes over your body."

He put one arm around his son and continued. "I was pretty mad when I saw the mess, but I'm not sure I have the right moral compass on this one, because you inherited your temper from me."

"But you don't get mad like that."

"Not now, but I did for a long time."

"Really?

"Yes."

"What stopped it?"

"Your mother. I realized I was going to lose her if I didn't find a way to control myself. So I just decided one day that I would never *ever* lose my temper again. And I haven't."

"Just like that?"

"Yes. Something like that only works when you have enough motivation. One day you'll find the right motivation. Until then, you have to do your best, but maybe it helps to know that I understand."

Jeremiah couldn't help but start to cry. It'd been a long time since he'd cried. He sobbed and then rubbed his eyes with his fists.

"What's Scott doing?"

"He's fine. I told him I'd buy him new cars to replace the ones you broke. He's looking forward to going shopping to do that." Then Dad smiled. "He'll have fun building them again."

* * *

The motivation Jeremiah needed to control his temper did not come quickly or easily, but after the talk with his father, he became more acutely aware of how he was different from the other boys.

None of them started fist fights, and even though Jeremiah started to notice that more directly, it didn't stop him from taking a shot at one of the kids at school at least once a week. It mattered not a whit that some of them were three grades above him and had thirty pounds that he didn't. When his temper flared, it made no difference.

His mother dutifully tended to his wounds and never commented on them. She knew he seemed to have little control, and maybe when she prayed at night, she added a little verse to ask God to help him.

Jeremiah loved to wander through the city. When he was younger, he'd often been scolded by his mom for leaving home to explore an area he hadn't seen yet or re-visit some favorite place, often the bank of the Cuyahoga River, about four blocks from his house. There was a bend there caused by eons of erosion, making the river look like a snake as it coiled through town.

He'd discovered a special spot on the river bank, by a big old oak tree with crazy roots crawling out of the ground. There was a flat spot between two roots where he could sit and watch the river flow by. It was quiet, and although he never felt lonely, he never saw anybody else.

Jeremiah called the place his "fort," even though there was no structure other than the tree. He didn't care. The tree was wrapped around behind him protectively, and he felt like the king of the world there.

Sometimes he'd almost be hypnotized by the lazy swirl of the water. On this particular day, his eyes were droopy and his brain empty, like he was drifting along with the current.

Then, out of nowhere, a cat jumped down from a branch above his head.

Jeremiah felt like a monster had jumped onto him, a big, black, rabid dog or a werewolf right from the Saturday afternoon *Thriller Chiller Theater* on Channel 6.

He jumped and screamed, and his mind reeled. He saw the animal and grabbed it. He wanted to fucking *kill* the thing before it could kill him. He grabbed the cat by the head and swung it, smashing it against the side of the tree.

The terror had turned into anger, wanting revenge for the cat scaring him. He threw the animal into the water.

Within seconds, the fear and anger had both left, and he watched as the cat, barely conscious, tried to paddle to the bank. A steady stream of blood drifted in the current behind it, and it was only a minute or so before Jeremiah lost sight of it.

He stared at where he last saw the cat.

"Are you okay?" he whispered.

Of course, he knew it wasn't.

He stared at his hands, as if they were responsible for him losing his temper.

He'd never hurt a defenseless animal, and he lowered his head in shame. After a moment he looked around, and for the first time he saw another person in his secret spot. His brother, Scott, was staring at him, mouth open.

"I didn't mean to . . . ," Jeremiah said.

Scott knew better, though. He'd been on the receiving end of Jeremiah's anger attacks too many times. He turned and ran.

"Scott! Wait!"

Jeremiah thought of chasing his brother, but he knew that would just scare Scott more. He sat on the ground in his fort and wanted to cry, but he couldn't.

He did shut his eyes and for the first time in his life, he prayed to a God he didn't really believe in.

After that day, Jeremiah taught himself control. He knew he'd crossed a line and never wanted to cross it again. For the most part, for a long time, he succeeded.

Chapter 6
1994

Jeremiah continued to focus his energies on learning magic. The more he learned, the more he loved it. He loved magic the way some kids loved baseball. He knew he was destined for the big leagues.

As a teenager, he worked on the basics. He became an expert palmist, and he mastered every card trick he could find. He pored over every magic book in the public library in detail. The books mostly taught card tricks and shell games, and although the kits he stole from the Toy and Game Emporium were a little more sophisticated, he knew there were many more complicated tricks he needed to learn.

He wanted to know everything.

All the while he was learning his craft, he also studied subjects at school that might possibly help him. He wasn't always sure how the different fields might help, but he had a sense that math was going to be important. Some of the books he read hinted at building boxes or other contraptions, and he would need to be able to figure out the precise sizes of each component. Carpentry wasn't taught in his school, but he took a general trades course that covered the basics, so he could cut wood without taking his finger off, and he learned how to sand and polish his projects to hide any secret joints.

He took acting classes and joined the debate team, figuring that the lessons he learned there would help when he was on stage and needed to keep an audience's attention.

Jeremiah soaked everything in. He was also careful not to screw up any of the other school subjects. History and geography might not fit into his future, but failing them would cause trouble with his parents, so he worked hard enough to end up with at least a B- in anything like that. For his core subjects, he demanded an A of himself.

As time went on, his parents started to realize the plan that Jeremiah was building for himself. At first they figured that this was just a phase and that by the time he graduated high school, their son would come to his senses and find a *real* career. So, they tolerated things. They never did know about the thefts, but they saw him reading dozens of books from the library, and he spent at least a couple of hours every night practicing.

Sometimes Jeremiah would arrange a private show for them, and he loved the look of amazement on their faces when he did something that should be impossible.

Jeremiah's favorite was a simple shell game. He'd have three shells on a table in front of him, with a little plastic pea beneath one. He'd move the shells around faster and faster, and ask his father where the pea was.

They must have done the same trick at least a hundred times over the course of a few years, sometimes several times in a row. His dad never once picked the right shell.

Of course, while Dad was watching the shells' movements, Jeremiah was watching his father's eyes. It was easy to see when he blinked or otherwise lost his concentration for just a split second, and that was when he would pull the switch and shift where the pea was.

"I still can't figure out how you do it," his father once said after three failed attempts in a row. "I've stopped following the damned thing and just guess now, and I still can't get it."

Jeremiah shrugged. "It's magic, Dad."

His dad smiled. "Not sure I buy that."

"What else could it be? Surely you'd end up picking the right choice by dumb luck once in a while, right?"

"I don't know . . ."

Luck only played a small part in Jeremiah's success. It was all in the eyes. If his dad was paying attention, Jeremiah waited for the right split second to switch the pea. Sometimes, though, his dad did glaze over and wait to pick a shell at random. In that case, Jeremiah would try to predict where he was going to guess. His dad sometimes would pick the same shell two times in a row but never three, so if the middle shell was picked twice, he knew it was safe to have the pea end up there on the next attempt. Other psychological tricks helped him guess what his dad would choose. And he never let him go on too long. Four times in a row was plenty, and only if most of those were honest (but hopeless) attempts to actually follow the pea.

Random choice was Jeremiah's least favorite game, so he'd cut off soon if he realized Dad was playing that way.

* * *

"Ready?"

Jeremiah peeked at the audience from behind the curtain.

"As ready as we'll ever be," he answered. "Right?"

He turned and looked at Suzette, his assistant.

"You're gonna kill them," she said.

"Looks like about six hundred people."

Jeremiah took a deep breath. They'd done a full dress rehearsal earlier that day, but they really had no idea how the show would go over in front of a real audience. At the rehearsal, they'd had about thirty people, mostly the people who worked at the theater and their friends.

This is it. My real life starts today, at age twenty.

He wanted to look out again, but that wouldn't settle his nerves.

"Everyone's set, right?" He knew that his voice sounded like he was pleading.

Suzette laughed and gave him a hug.

"Just think. This is what you've wanted your entire life. All those people paid twenty bucks to watch you do your show. They're going to love it."

He nodded and glanced around. He could see the other two helpers, girls like Suzette, hired three weeks ago after Jeremiah had walked to the local unemployment office. They looked bored.

"Don't worry about them," Suzette said after seeing where he was looking. "They're just window dressing."

He nodded. Suzette and the other girls wore sparkly red skirts and tops. On their backs was a stylized letter J with a white dove launching from the top.

Jeremiah knew that Suzette wanted long-term employment and was doing everything she could to make that happen. That's why she ended up being his assistant while the others were more or less window dressing.

She'd also hit on him once, but he politely deflected it. She was pretty enough, but not really what he was looking for. One day, he knew he'd find the girl of his dreams. For now, magic was his mistress.

The stage manager called, "Two minutes! Places everyone!" He was a frumpy, middle-aged man who had only a tiny role tonight; he got Jeremiah on stage, and then at the end of the night, he got him off.

There was a lighting guy, a music guy, and even a guy who took care of the curtains. There were ushers and ticket sellers, and at the front of the theater was a bar stocked with a healthy supply of beer and wine. Jeremiah was grateful about that, figuring that a well-lubricated audience would be an appreciative one.

After a cheesy local comedian had spent twenty minutes warming up the audience, Jeremiah took his mark in the wings.

Clouded by the curtains, he heard the words he'd wanted to hear for the past ten years.

Please welcome the master magician, Jeremiah Moore!

The curtain raised and Jeremiah felt a rush of excitement course through him. The audience was cheering . . . and it was for him.

He showed his broad smile, the smile he'd been practicing since he was a little kid, and he walked to center stage.

A stark bright light blinded him. He was prepared for the spotlight, having had it aimed at him during the dress rehearsal, but it was still unnerving to hear the audience applaud and not see a single person. He pulled his cane from the hidden slot in his pants, making it appear to have jumped into his right hand from nowhere, tossing a spray of fireworks to his left as he did so.

The audience gasped at the fireworks, and as they fizzled out, the spotlight slowly dimmed while the more general stage lights arose, so Jeremiah could finally see his first audience.

His heart was pounding with excitement, and he puffed his chest out in pride.

"Thank you!" he shouted. His voice croaked a bit. He was wearing a thin wire microphone and the acoustics of the wonderful old theater carried his voice to the back. He knew from the earlier sound checks that each person in the audience would hear his every whisper.

"It's wonderful to be in Boise in the great state of Idaho! I feel like you've all been so welcoming to me and my team. And I hope that tonight I can repay some of the gracious hospitality I've seen in the past couple of days."

The audience clapped politely.

From the wings, the three girls hurried out, two on his right, Suzette on his left. Suzette attached a cape, suspended by invisible wires, around Jeremiah's neck. Jeremiah bowed and then ran toward the front of the stage and jumped as if off a diving board. Several people in the first few rows screamed before Jeremiah started to fly, just like Superman, around the audience.

The cheers got louder as he reached the back of the theater and turned to head back to the stage.

This is my life, he thought as he grinned down to his audience.

Over the course of the next hour, Jeremiah played out some of his best tricks. He did small magic (card tricks were still among his favorites) and large (various ways of making his assistants disappear).

He loved it. It was a night he would never forget.

Suzette was clearly enjoying the attention, too, gleefully beaming at the end of each trick. The other girls blended into the background, but that was okay.

Jeremiah watched as the girls rolled two large wooden cases on stage, pushing them together to form a coffin-like box. Then he grabbed Suzette, now dressed like a captive in scruffy shorts and a ripped T-shirt, surrounded by chains. He pulled on the chain, seeming to drag her against her will into the casket, snapping her feet into blocks that kept her from moving. At the other end of the cases, he pulled the chains, forcing her arms out of two small holes, then closed the tops of the cases and shut them.

The helpers turned the case in circles, showing that there was nothing beneath.

Then Jeremiah brought out the chain saw.

The trick was nothing special. Most people had seen a girl supposedly cut in half before on TV, but he knew that, in person, it was still one of the more effective tricks.

Suzette only had a few seconds to twist her feet, slip her legs out of their trap, and to pull her legs up to her chest before the saw came down.

And she had no way to tell Jeremiah if there was a problem. As with all tricks of this type, both magician and assistant knew the risks and practiced many hours without the saw to make sure nothing would go wrong.

This time, though, maybe the bright lights slowed her reaction, or the audience murmurs hypnotized her. Nobody would ever know. The blood spewing up on the chain saw was the first sign of disaster.

Jeremiah yanked the saw up and stared aghast at the blood spilling down.

"Oh my God," he said. He stared to the left of the stage. "Get the doctor!"

Two stage hands came running out and pulled the casket behind the curtain. Suzette was screaming in pain.

Silence enveloped Jeremiah. He stared at the audience, not seeming to have control of his body. Shortly, the curtain fell, separating him from the six hundred people who had just watched him cut his chainsaw into his assistant.

* * *

Suzette was in the hospital for two weeks. She hadn't been able to free her feet in time, and the chain saw had cut deeply into her thighs. The doctor who was on hand for the show had been able to staunch most of the bleeding, and he gave her a shot for the pain.

At the hospital, they patched her up, but one bone was chipped and she needed two transfusions to get her blood levels back to normal. Physical therapy slowly helped get her back on her feet.

Jeremiah only visited her one time, the day after the accident. Suzette's mother and father were also visiting, and they tried to convince him to leave.

"No," said Suzette. "It was my fault. I wasn't fast enough."

"I'm so sorry," Jeremiah said.

Her father was biting his lip, his face red with anger. Jeremiah knew he'd just as soon punch him as look at him.

"I've told the administrators that I'll cover the bill."

"I would certainly hope so," whispered Suzette's mother.

The bill was $48,000. At the time, Jeremiah had $485.03 in his bank account. At the age of twenty, it seemed that his magical career was over.

Chapter 7
2012

Alannah Clark loved Seattle. It'd been four years since she and Savannah had left upstate New York and followed I-90 to the west coast. Although they had no notion where they'd end up (well, truth be told, Alannah knew that *she* had no clue, but sometimes Savannah surprised her with plans Alannah had no idea about), they hopped out of their last hitch-hiked ride in downtown Seattle, and when they climbed out and Alannah smelled the salty Puget Sound, she knew she never wanted to leave.

They found a temporary place to stay at a youth hostel and then rented a basement apartment a few miles from the core of the city.

A week after *that* they had a job. A shared job, because their rent was low enough and they could afford to live quite easily on one salary.

The job application, interview, and other hiring steps were all done using the Internet. There were actually two interviews, one with some flunky in Human Resources and the other with a manager in the Call Center. The single job was supposedly for Savannah, but they just took turns. Who would ever know? Or care?

It was the perfect job as far as Alannah was concerned. They were Customer Service Representatives for Millipad, a reseller of Apple iPads and other computer equipment. The entire business was virtual, with no store front, no factory, no sales team, no board rooms. Everyone from the CEO on down worked from their own homes. The company had almost no expenses other than salaries, allowing them to charge lower prices, compared to their competition.

Savannah (or Alannah, with no one being the wiser) was expected to answer one hundred customer calls over seven and a half hours. Every person she talked to was subsequently e-mailed a survey. As long as her customers were happy and she met her daily quote, nobody from the company would ever bother her.

It was perfect.

* * *

Alannah stretched her arms and clicked her phone off for the end of her shift. She could see the counter at the bottom of her screen showing that she'd helped 121 customers today. She yawned, feeling a buzz in her head from the sudden silence after talking on the phone all day. She placed her headset on the desk and stood to stretch.

A quiet Wednesday in May, she thought. *Time to go for it.*

She sipped the glass of water she kept on her desk and then walked to the apartment door. She locked the door behind her and headed across the street and down a block to a small strip mall.

She was nervous. Her entire life she'd been the nervous one, tentative, shy, and introverted. Talking on the phone was one thing, but this was a big step.

It was cool out, but she was wearing a sweater and jogging pants so that didn't bother her.

The strip mall wasn't new, but it was convenient for picking up groceries and (from Savannah's perspective) the occasional bottle of wine.

Alannah walked quickly to the dance studio that had opened three months earlier. She'd been too chicken to go any sooner. Today was the day she'd forced herself to find the courage.

The business had an open reception area. From the door, Alannah could see three studios where dance lessons would be taught, glass-walled so parents could watch the children's lessons. Curtains inside each classroom provided privacy for adult lessons.

"Can I help you? You look lost."

There was a woman behind the counter in front of Alannah.

"Hi. I'm—"

She hesitated, all of a sudden not so sure this was a good idea.

"It's okay. I don't bite."

"I'm just not sure what I want," whispered Alannah. She could feel her heart beating, and her head felt light.

"Honey, I've been hunting for a decade to find out what *I* want. At the moment, it's running this place. Don't ask me to tell you if I'd give you the same answer in another ten years."

She laughed loudly, and for a moment, Alannah felt jealous that the woman could be so comfortable with a complete stranger. She nodded and bit her lip. *This was a really bad idea.*

The woman came over and reached out her hand. "I'm Nickie. Owner, teacher, receptionist, accounting . . . pretty much the whole ball of wax."

"My name is Alannah. I've always wanted to study dance."

She smiled, but it was forced.

"Never taken any classes? How old are you?"

"Twenty. Well, I will be in two months. No, no lessons. I guess you'd say I'm self-taught."

"Well, let's see what you've got. Ballet? Jazz?"

"More just a modern mix. I'm not really sure what you'd call it. I've just kind of thrown things together."

Nickie walked with her to the closest classroom. There were mats on one half of the room, while the rest was naked hardwood. She waved her hand, indicating that Alannah could pick whichever side she wanted.

The room smelled faintly of sweat. Alannah took off her sweater and jogging pants. Beneath, she wore a black leotard.

She took a long breath, trying to convince herself not to run away.

"Take your time, sweetie. I'm not in a hurry. I don't have a class for another hour. I'm here early every day, but mostly I just push paper around."

Alannah stared at the teacher, eyes big and bright. She nodded and walked to the hardwood side of the floor before turning back.

"Do you have music?"

"Oh, of course."

Nickie pranced to a corner of the room where a small A/V center was set up. She looked at the setup and pressed some buttons.

"'Time of My Life.' That okay?"

Alannah nodded. She remembered watching *Dirty Dancing* and loving the song.

As the music started, she closed her eyes and started to nod to the beat. She lifted her arms from her sides and rose onto her toes as she gently promenaded to the middle of the room. Her face tilted from one side to the other and back and then she stopped, reached up toward the ceiling, stretching as far as she could.

The music changed to a faster pace and along with it, Alannah ran to the far end of the room, swiveled, and then started a series of cartwheels, four in a row, before doing a flip without touching the floor at all. She landed solidly on her feet and reversed, doing several backward flips.

When the music slowed again, she fell to her knees and pantomimed reaching above her to some unseen entity. Emotions poured from her face as she went through her routine: love, fear, hatred, sadness, and joy. Each of these expressions was perfect, and she knew it.

She slowly rose to her feet and leaned over backward, bending until her hands touched the floor just behind her feet. With no apparent effort, she lifted her legs and flipped over to land normally.

She spun in a pirouette, her arms gracefully touching above her head. Twists, spirals, and glides followed, as she mixed in some jazz movements.

Alannah almost forgot Nickie was there. She was dancing only for herself, the safest place she'd found in her entire life.

The music continued, and she pushed herself and her abilities, wanting to try new moves and new ways to show her buried emotions, and with every move she made, she felt the music deep inside her heart, and she lived her real life.

* * *

The music was stopped for almost twenty seconds before Nickie finally spoke. "Wow. You learned all that yourself?"

Alannah nodded. Her forehead was glistening with sweat, but she hadn't thought to bring a towel and she didn't want to wipe it away with her arm, so she tried to ignore it.

"My parents couldn't afford lessons, so I watched sometimes. Through windows, just like what you have here. I watched how other people learned, and I tried to do some of the same moves. I'd go to the school gym after class, but only on days when there were no sporting events. I'd have the place all to myself lots of times."

"You're very thin."

Nickie walked over and stared at Alannah.

"I don't condone eating disorders."

Alannah laughed. "Don't worry, that's not me. I just have a lucky metabolism. I can eat pizza, McDonald's hamburgers, steaks, or whatever else I want and my weight always manages to hover right around 110. I'm five foot two, but I love eating. I'm just one of the fortunate ones who don't put pounds on."

Nickie kept staring.

"And my sister is the same," Alannah continued. "We're twins and we're both skinny. My mother was the same."

Nickie nodded. "Let's talk about what we want to do with you." She smiled and took Alannah back to the reception area.

They sat in cozy armchairs facing each other and worked out a training schedule.

* * *

Savannah Clark also adored living in Seattle, almost as much as her sister. She loved not having to deal with snow and ice over the winter, not having to deal with frigid temperatures, and for that matter, not having to deal with the stifling heat of East Coast summers.

The rain got to her sometimes, but it wasn't a big deal. She would imagine the rain turning to snow and, all of a sudden, it wasn't a big deal any more.

The job-sharing with Alannah was working perfectly. Savannah didn't mind the job, but listening to people complain on the phone all day was a little difficult, so alternating days with sis kept them both sane.

Savannah also liked the freedom that having their own apartment provided. The day after Alannah found the dance studio, Savannah finished work and then stared at the small white board she'd attached to her bedroom wall, which listed the letters A through Z in her neatest handwriting. There were names beside twelve of them: Alex, Cody, Dennis, Franklin, George, Jack, Norman, Otis, Paul, Timothy, Victor, and Walter.

Fourteen more and I'll have the whole set.

Savannah smiled. Collecting men wasn't normally considered a wholesome hobby, but what the heck. She liked to fuck. She'd started the list on New Year's Day, four months ago.

She glanced at the group again, knowing it would be hard to find a Quentin or an Xavier, but . . . she had eight more months in the year.

Dinner that night consisted of fried wieners cut up and mixed with a box of Kraft Dinner. She scarfed it down with a Coke and tossed the dishes in the dishwasher. It was only half full, but she started it anyhow. Alannah would unload it when she got around to it.

The closest bar was two blocks away, but she'd been there a lot lately and felt like a change. She found another one ten minutes in the other direction.

The next morning she wanted to add Nick to her white board but she already had an N. She shrugged and wrote his middle name, Martin.

* * *

A month later, Savannah sat on the toilet and shook her head.
"No, can't be . . ."
But it was. She held the little plastic stick in her hand, and the bright red line told her she was pregnant, that missing her period wasn't some weird fluke.
"But I can't be . . ."
Three days later, her doctor confirmed that she'd be expecting a baby sometime near Christmas. She didn't know who the father was.

That night she cried herself to sleep and felt lonelier than she had ever imagined. She wrote about her feelings in the diary she shared with Alannah. She talked about her fears, her despair, her humiliation, and most of all, her uncertainty.
"I don't know what to do," she wrote.
Alannah did.

The next day, Savannah found a brochure on the dining room table that talked about how to make the choice she faced. She read the notes and made a list of pros and cons. She wrote them all in her diary.

Three weeks later, the baby was gone. Savannah knew it was the right decision, but that didn't make it any easier. Part of her felt like she'd lost a connection she might never have again. Her baby was gone. Nobody would ever know what special abilities he or she might have developed, nor what kind of bond they could have had with their mother.

Savannah cried more than ever, but she eventually stopped and decided that she needed to move on with her life.

She erased the white board and took it off the wall.

In her diary, she wrote, "Thank you," knowing that her sister would read it one day.

Part 2

The Magic Show

"It is the unspoken ethic of all magicians to not reveal the secrets."

—David Copperfield

Chapter 8
2014

Jeremiah Moore celebrated his fortieth birthday by finding a new place to live, moving to Seattle after ten years in San Francisco. It wasn't that he had anything against the city, not exactly. He just felt antsy (a word he got from his grandmother, who, when Jeremiah was young, used to say he must have ants in his pants). He had visited Seattle many years ago and had fond memories of sitting on a park bench overlooking Lake Washington. He remembered walking to Pike Place, visiting the first Starbucks, watching fish being tossed fifty feet in the middle of the market amid the oohs and ahhs of dozens of fascinated tourists . . . and the seed was planted that finally grew fruit.

He'd been searching for the right apartment all day, checking web sites on his iPhone for places to rent, but nothing had appealed to him until he found the loft above the small strip mall.

At first he thought nothing of it. Who wanted to live above a strip mall? As he looked around, though, he realized it would be awfully convenient. The mall had anything he'd need. Since he would be spending the majority of his time at home, practicing and perfecting his work, that was a definite plus.

The apartment itself was the clincher, though. The ad had described it as a one bedroom with a large living area but he saw it differently.

"Might be too much space for a single fella."

The realtor led Jeremiah up to the second floor and showed him the space. He glanced at the bedroom on one side, not really caring about it. On the other side, a kitchen held the usual assortment of appliances. He ignored that, too, other than to mentally check off a box.

But, the main room . . .

It was easily thirty feet wide and ten deep. The ceiling was ten feet above the floor.

"My stage," he whispered.

"Beg pardon?"

Jeremiah smiled at the realtor. "It's perfect."

"Well, good to hear. You know the rent from the ad, so if you want it, I just need first and last month and a damage deposit."

"Why is it so big?"

"Guess it's to match the size of the dance studio below. Maybe originally an overflow area? Not my business, but that's my figuring."

Jeremiah walked to the center of the large room. The floor consisted of two-inch wide strips of hardwood. He thought maybe oak, but he wasn't sure. It wasn't all shiny and new, but it was hardwood just the same.

He held his arms out and imagined the audience in front of him. There was plenty of room all around him.

"I'll take it."

* * *

His equipment arrived three days later, filling a sixteen-foot, cubical moving truck. The official weight was 2,840 pounds, of which the vast majority was paraphernalia for his show. At the beginning of his career he never would have imagined having more than a ton of magic equipment, but there it was.

There was no elevator, since he was only one floor up, so that certainly made the movers work for their money. When everything had been delivered to the second floor, he gave each of the two movers a fifty-dollar tip. They thanked him and they left.

Jeremiah loved his new digs. He spent the rest of the day moving things around and unpacking boxes. He thought of playing some music but decided against it. The sound of boxes scraping across the floor boards was all he wanted to hear.

He only had two chairs, both better suited to a lawn party. When he had moved all his boxes to generally where they belonged, he cracked a Coors Light and sat.

"And the magic begins again in a new venue," he said, toasting an invisible audience.

He rested his eyes and enjoyed being in his new home.

An hour later, Jeremiah realized his stomach was rumbling. He hadn't eaten any lunch and it was now almost 7:00 p.m.

"One advantage of living at a strip mall," he said.

He rubbed his eyes and took one last look at the apartment before heading out.

At one end of the mall was the unusually named Wilson's Chinese, while at the other was the Swiss Kitchen, a chain of mid-scale family restaurants.

He chose the Kitchen and walked over. The smell of rotisserie chicken wafted everywhere, making him realize he was *starving*.

The restaurant was mostly empty. He assumed the families ate earlier, which was good to know for future times when he might want to eat in silence.

"Can I bring you a drink, sir?"

The waitress gave him a bright smile, and he returned it. *Seems like a friendly place*, he thought. *I like it.*

"Just a coffee would be great. Thanks."

"First time here?"

"How would you know that?"

"I—" She shrugged and laughed. "I guess I've worked here too long. I know all the regulars." She looked around at the other waitresses. "We all do."

"Ahh."

"Sorry, I didn't mean to be rude or anything."

"No, it's fine. You're right. This is my first time here. I've just moved into the apartment above the dance studio."

"Well then, welcome to the neighborhood! I'm Errin Elizabeth and I'll be your server tonight."

"Nice to meet you, Errin Elizabeth."

She locked eyes with him and blushed. He couldn't help notice her nice smile, her long dark hair that curled at the ends, and the way she glanced at his left ring finger, which was empty.

He nodded and said, "Coffee would be great." Then he lifted the menu, still glancing in her direction.

"I'll be back," she said.

Jeremiah watched her leave before returning his attention to the menu. As with other women he had met, he didn't feel any sparks, and he somehow knew he never would. Errin was pleasant, and she'd be happy if he asked her out, but he also knew it would come to nothing. He'd seen that movie too many times.

Quarter chicken with a skewer of shrimp, he read. *Two choices of sides, $16.95.*

His stomach approved his choice, rumbling again.

He left Errin Elizabeth a 20% tip and thanked her for the kind welcome. He promised to return soon, and he meant it.

* * *

Back at the apartment that night, he spent a couple more hours organizing his belongings.

He was careful as he unpacked his books and set them up in his small shelves. He only had a couple of dozen print books, mostly classics he'd read over and over again, including both *Romeo and Juliet* and *West Side Story*. Jeremiah craved the kind of love that both stories showed him. He knew, however, it was very unlikely to ever fall his way.

After all, he thought, *it took Shakespeare to write romance like that. Nobody ever found it in real life.*

He still hoped for one day, though. His heart wanted to find a soul mate. She was out there somewhere . . . wasn't she?

His other books included *The Grapes of Wrath*, *The Shining*, *The Old Man and the Sea*, *The Andromeda Strain*, *Pride and Prejudice*, and *The Hunger Games*. He liked what he liked, and if nobody else could understand why they all belonged on his shelf, well, he wouldn't lose any sleep.

What would surprise people more, though, was the lack of books about his craft. There was only one: *The Encyclopedia of Magic*.

He actually owned hundreds of other books on magic, but they were all stored on his Kindle. He didn't treasure them the way he treasured the print books he owned.

When the books were arranged exactly as he wanted them, Jeremiah stripped to his briefs and climbed into his double-sized bed. That night, as always, he dreamed of magic and love.

* * *

The next morning, he woke with a renewed sense of purpose. He sat on the edge of his bed and stared at the wall. Several framed photos of people leaned against the wall. Jeremiah planned to hang them sometime in the next day or two.

Three of the photos were of his mom, his dad, and both of them at their wedding. He loved how the photographer had captured them glancing at each other with a secret smile as they met at the front of the church.

A few feet from those photos was one more, a picture of Suzette, grinning widely. Before the accident had sliced her leg.

Suzette never knew that he had that photo and that he used it every day to remind himself that no part of his act was as important as safety. It'd taken him five years to pay her hospital bill, and he had never contacted her again after he saw her that one time while she was recovering.

It was two years after the accident before he finally had the courage to once again perform magic in public, and to this day, he still hadn't tried to cut a woman in half. Every day, though, he felt closer to being able to take that challenge. He knew that with the right precautions (and the right assistant), the trick was safe.

One day . . .

* * *

For two weeks, Jeremiah worked on setting up his apartment, which consisted mostly of hundreds of individual pieces of equipment for his magic show.

His next booking was for a week-long stint in Orlando, and he wanted to shift around some of his tricks to appeal to a younger audience. He loved performing in front of teens and pre-teens, because lots of them came in expecting a stupid waste of time.

Instead they found themselves marveling as Jeremiah performed miracle after miracle, and almost every one of them walked away believing in magic. Real magicians could even beat Walt Disney World. They'd be return customers for life, wondering how he did the things he did.

The expressions on kids' faces were more rewarding than the pay checks he received.

The two weeks passed in a flash, blinked away like one of his doves.

In that time, he got to know the little strip mall well. He alternated meals at the Chinese restaurant and the Swiss Kitchen, and he already knew both menus. He could smell the Chinese food every time he left his apartment.

He also knew every one of the Starbucks baristas, the clerks at the small grocery store and the specialty wine store, and even the owner of the dance studio below his loft. Nickie was a nice enough woman, and Jeremiah had chatted with her once as she was arriving at the studio. She was the owner and, yes, the apartment he was renting was originally part of the studio. Her dreams were bigger than her number of customers, though, and she scaled it back to the single floor.

Jeremiah hesitated as he left the apartment, not really wanting either restaurant choice tonight. He glanced to the busy street beyond the parking lot. Maybe it was time to go hunting for a different place . . . .

Just then, a woman walked in front of him as she made her way to the dance studio door. She glanced at him and gave him a closed-mouth smile that was both sincere and guarded.

She was absolutely beautiful.

Wow.

Before he knew what he was doing, he blurted out, "Hi there."

Oh, Jesus, he thought. *What am I doing?*

That one smile had captured him. Somehow he knew that that single image would live in his brain forever. It was a snapshot from Instagram or Facebook that he would never forget.

In the split second before she turned toward the studio, he saw her soul.

He saw her almond-shaped green eyes that widened just a fraction. He saw the corners of her perfect mouth rise and her nose wiggle a fraction of an inch. He saw the life in her bouncing dark hair and the scattering of tiny freckles on her cheeks.

She was the most beautiful girl he'd ever seen.

And when she glanced back after he called to her, he knew immediately that they couldn't possibly have a future together. She looked like she was barely twenty, and he was twice that age.

She smiled again, this time a broad smile full of bright white teeth.

"Hi."

Her voice was whispery, shy, full of secrets and promises, and Jeremiah knew his heart was lost.

The girl stopped and looked at him, as if she was trying to see if he was somebody she knew. Why else would he have said hi to her?

"I'm . . ."

He stopped and shook his head. His mind wasn't working. He licked his lips and tried again.

"I'm the tenant from upstairs. My name is Jeremiah."

"Hi," she said again. Her voice was soft and gentle, and Jeremiah's heart felt her shyness and knew immediately this girl was fragile and needed to be treasured.

He lurched his hand out, startling her a bit. She recovered and reluctantly shook his hand.

"I'm Alannah," she said. "I practice here. Dance."

"Yes, I kind of figured that. It being a dance studio and all."

She laughed.

"I guess so," she said.

"What kind of dance do you do?"

Alannah lowered her head as if she was ashamed and didn't answer for a moment. When she did, she kept her head low.

"I don't really follow a style. It's just what I like to do."

"That sounds very creative."

She looked up and locked eyes with him.

"You know about dance?"

"Not as much as I should. I'm an entertainer. A magician, actually. I've shared the stage with a lot of people over the years: singers, comedians, and dancers."

"What kind of magic do you do?"

He shrugged. "I don't really follow a style. It's just what I like to do."

Alannah's face reddened and stepped backward.

"You're making fun of me."

"Oh my God, I'm sorry. I didn't mean it like that at all. I really liked your answer."

"I should go."

"Can I watch?"

"What?"

"Can I watch you practice?"

She stared at him, pursing her lips. He wondered if she was considering running away or calling the cops. She was tense. He smiled and tried to reassure her with his charm.

Don't leave me now. It's taken my whole life to find you.

"Sure, why not."

He let out a long breath, without even knowing he had been holding it.

"Thank you."

"Don't make fun of me."

Chapter 9
2014

Alannah slept that night, totally relaxed. She'd written in her diary about the stranger who wanted to watch her dance. Even though he was much older than she, she felt attracted to him. She'd never have the courage to tell him that, of course, but as she drifted off to sleep, his face stayed in her imagination. She liked that.

She wasn't very experienced with men; her perpetual shyness was a big part of that. That's what made him such a nice surprise.

Chances were that she'd never see him again, but that didn't stop her from contemplating what might be.

"A agua esta fria."

What?

She blinked awake and froze in her bed. The voice seemed too real to have been a dream. And it was that odd phrase again that she'd heard once before in a—

(vision)

—dream. It was the same soft voice, a girl or perhaps a young boy.

Alannah sat up and realized her fingers and hands were sticky. She couldn't see anything in the dark, so she shuffled her way to the bathroom and flicked the light on.

Her hands were covered in blood. It was sticky, but not wet, like it'd been there a little while.

Oh my God . . .

Alannah's first reaction was that she must be bleeding somewhere, but she didn't feel any pain, and other than some dried red smudges on her night clothes, there was no blood anywhere except on her hands. She wanted to cry out but she was frozen with fear.

"What happened?"

She clenched her fists. The blood was tacky and sticky, but there was no pain. She glanced toward her bedroom, but there was only darkness.

Pulling together every bit of courage she could find, she turned the water on and scrubbed the blood from her hands. It swirled down the sink and left her with just wet, cold fingers.

Part of her knew she needed to turn the damned bedroom light on and see what there was to see, but she ignored that. She wanted to stay hidden in the bathroom as long as she could. It was safe there.

Surely there was nobody hiding in her room.

Who's blood was it?

She bent over and splashed water on her face, hoping that the chill would help wake her up and allow her to think about what to do.

Alannah listened, but there were no strange noises from her bedroom.

She grabbed a hand towel, patted her face dry, and looked at the mirror.

It wasn't her face staring back. It was a little boy. He had long, light brown hair and was naked. His face and body were bloated, parts of his flesh ripped off. A large hole disfigured his right cheek, and blood oozed out of it.

His face was pure evil, hate lasering from his eyes and hunger from his mouth.

She couldn't move, knowing she must be dreaming, but this wasn't like any dream she'd ever had. This felt real, and although she *wanted* it to be a dream, her mind screamed no.

He was real.

The boy grinned hugely. His teeth were covered with green slime.

Alannah's legs almost gave out, and she grabbed onto the counter to stop herself from falling.

"*A agua esta fria!*" he shouted.

"No," Alannah whispered. "You're not real."

The boy laughed and said, "Oh, I'm real, sis. And I'm coming back."

Alannah couldn't look at him. Neither could she move. She wanted to leave the bathroom but couldn't. Her legs wouldn't carry her; neither could she move her hands. She couldn't even turn her head from the monster staring at her.

The boy laughed and reached for her. She felt sure that his arms would come right out of the mirror to strangle her.

She couldn't scream, couldn't move, could barely think. She was a frozen statue of herself. Urine spilled down her legs.

All she could do was close her eyes. She didn't want to see him touching her.

"Who are you?" she wanted to ask, but no sound came from her mouth.

After a moment, she gasped as she realized she hadn't been breathing. Her eyes flew open, and she saw only her own terrified image in the glass.

Her body was free again, and she almost collapsed but caught herself on the counter.

Alannah took a deep breath, not daring to move her eyes from the messy girl in the mirror. Her hair was soaked, and the T-shirt she wore was covered in sweat. Her eyes were wide and tearstains glistened below them.

"You're not real," she said again. She wasn't sure if she was saying it to herself or to the little boy.

She walked back to her bedroom and turned the light on.

Blood stains marked the sheets where her hands had been.

She sat on the side of the bed, thoughts of Jeremiah Moore long gone.

Would Savannah know anything?

No. The blood was still wet when I woke. Fresh.

Alannah creeped herself out by kneeling and looking under her bed. There was nobody there. Her room was exactly as it should be, except for the bloody sheets.

She walked through their apartment, but there were no signs of anybody. The door was closed, locked, and deadlocked. The windows were shut and locked.

She bit her lower lip. There was no way anyone could have gotten into their place and certainly no way for them to have left without leaving something unlocked.

Everything was quiet, and although Alannah normally loved that, right now it felt somehow wrong.

It was 4:42 a.m.

She'd be waking up in less than an hour, so she decided to just stay awake. There was no way she would be able to get back to sleep, anyhow. She made coffee and sat in the living room, watching CNN with the volume turned low.

As she sat there, the odd phrase crept into her mind, but this time she thought she knew how it was spelled. She typed *A agua esta fria* into Google on her iPhone.

The water is cold.

Alannah frowned as she stared at the words translated from Portuguese.

"What water?"

Google didn't have an answer for that.

* * *

At a little before 6:00 a.m., sunshine started to stream through the apartment windows. Alannah had finished three cups of coffee (one more than she would usually drink in an entire day). She'd continued to watch CNN but none of the stories really sank in.

She swirled the mug in her hand, the last slurps of coffee waiting for her, but she decided she'd had enough and took it to the kitchen.

Wine would be better, she thought. She choked out a small laugh. She wasn't much of a drinker; Savannah would have more seriously gone that route.

Savannah.

She needed to know.

Alannah removed her diary from the bureau and wrote two entries. The first was about the vision she'd had of the scary little boy.

The second, longer, entry was about Jeremiah Moore. She took her time with this one, writing every detail she could remember about their meeting.

There was something about him . . .

For the first time since waking, she moved the Portuguese boy to the back of her mind and thought of something else. Some*one* else.

She liked his smile and his voice. She knew without a doubt that he was gentle and trustworthy and lovable. His smile was a wide grin that seemed to stretch too far, but it had made her want to kiss him.

He was taller than she (well, who wasn't?), probably by a foot, but that wouldn't matter, would it?

The age, though.

She tried to guess his age and decided he must be near forty. She was twenty-two.

"Not quite double."

It wouldn't make sense that he would be interested in her. He'd see her as a little kid. She was kidding herself to think he might be interested.

But would he be?

She went to her bedroom and took off her T-shirt and panties, tossing them in the laundry hamper for Sunday's chores.

After walking to the bathroom, she turned the shower on and climbed in. The water felt brisk and hot, and she was glad it would wash away any remnants of the blood.

She turned her back to the streaming water, letting it flow into her long dark hair. Her eyes were closed, and it felt nice.

"Wish you were joining me, Mr. Jeremiah."

She felt her face flush at that thought.

She finished her shower and got dressed. It was her day to work, so she poured herself one last coffee and sat at her desk, ready for the first call of the day.

Chapter 10
2014

Savannah Clark had decided to change her ways, but that oath lasted only two months. Every once in a while she thought of the baby that had lived inside her for a short time almost two years ago, and a kind of sadness came over her. She wanted it to be a *real* sadness, because she thought that was what she should feel, but it had happened so quickly that it was more like watching a melancholy movie. Still, she knew that she never wanted to go through that again.

However, she wasn't strong-willed.

Three days after her twin had seen a ten-year-old boy as her own reflection, Savannah woke up in a strange bedroom with a man she didn't know snoring beside her. Her head was pounding, and she vaguely remembered being at a bar the night before.

She slipped out of bed, naked, and looked for her clothes in the dim lighting. There were no lights on, but the morning haze drifted through a window.

"Ouch," she said as pain throbbed through her head. They'd been downing shooters at the bar—that much she remembered. But his name, or where they were? Nothing.

She saw her clothes piled near a chair and wasted no time getting herself dressed. Her watch was with her clothes, and she could see it was shortly after 5:00 a.m. Her purse was there, too.

"God, I think it's my day to work . . . ." She thought it was Tuesday, and paused to question herself.

Yup. My day.

Savannah tiptoed out of the bedroom and down a hall. She was in a two-bedroom apartment, but she didn't take much time to see if there was anything she might remember. She headed for the door and quietly let herself out.

The apartment was on the fifth floor, somewhere in downtown Seattle. When she ran to the street, she could see a hotel a block away, so she walked there. A taxi stand had three cars with drivers who were almost asleep. She hopped into the first cab in line and asked the driver to take her home.

When she arrived, Savannah took a fast shower and toasted a bagel. She slathered it with cream cheese and started a pot of coffee.

Six-fifteen. She still had forty-five minutes before she needed to get on the phones and answer inane questions from customers.

It'd been two days since she'd been home.

"What's new with you, sis?" she asked.

Savannah pulled out their shared diary and started to read.

Five minutes later, she stared at the words, finding them hard to imagine.

> The boy staring back at me looked dead. He was a ghost or a zombie or something and I was never so scared in my entire life. It should have been *my* fucking reflection!
>
> How is that possible?
>
> It's not.

Savannah stared at the words, and just for a second she wondered if Alannah was playing a trick on her, but, of course, that wouldn't be like her at all.

She also read all about Alannah meeting the stranger at the dance studio, and that intrigued her as much as the impossible reflection.

"Sounds like you have a little crush, Sis . . . ."

In the short time she had left before starting work, she wrote her own entry in the diary. Unlike her sister, though, she didn't feel compelled to tell the whole truth. She did admit to going out drinking, but in the journal it was with June Sophit, a friend a few blocks away. According to her new entry in the diary, Savannah stayed overnight at June's place.

She shrugged. What Alannah doesn't know wouldn't hurt her. With her coffee cup re-filled, she settled at her desk and sat cross-legged. The computer booted up for her, and she clicked the VPN icon to sign in to the main computer at Millipad. At exactly 7:00, she changed her status to AVAILABLE, and the first call came within ten seconds.

The job was sometimes boring, sometimes stressful, and always headache-inducing. Savannah knew the Millipad products inside and out from her training and was rarely stumped by a question. The stress only came when a client screamed over the phone about some perceived slight. Sometimes there was little to be done other than stay silent and let the person rant. She couldn't help somebody who wasn't being civil. When those calls came, it was almost always the customer's problem. They didn't follow the proper installation instructions or they deleted a program they shouldn't have or it was some other easily-explainable problem. It was just tough dealing with them when they were being irrational.

Starting the day with a hangover headache didn't help matters, but that started to fade soon enough. Over the course of the next eight hours, she talked to 116 customers. At 3:00 she finished with the current caller (a man who had accidentally hit the buy button twice but didn't want two tablets in his shopping cart), and set her status to NOT AVAILABLE.

One more day down.

She logged off and put her headset aside before stretching her legs. She made another bagel with cream cheese and washed it down with some milk.

The diary was still on the kitchen table where she'd left it. She thought again about the weird image of the dead little boy who had scared Alannah.

"Must be your imagination, Sis."

She put the diary away and grabbed a back pack. It was pink, a color she was not the slightest bit fond of, but she'd found it at a garage sale for five bucks. She made a tuna sandwich and a hardboiled egg and packed them along with two bottles of apple juice.

She liked the walk. The air was brisk, the sun shining, and the temperature a nice eighty-two degrees. She wished Seattle could be like that every day of the year.

The meal program wasn't called a soup kitchen, but that's how Savannah thought of it in her mind. It was officially called Seattle Volunteer Food Mission, but somehow that felt stilted and she liked the simpler phrase better. She walked to the side of the church and wandered around to the area in the back. The Mission was fairly small, but it fed dozens of homeless people every night.

Savannah recognized many of the people as she dished out a meal for them. Tonight, it was a helping of roast beef and potatoes, with a small cup of cream of mushroom soup. She was responsible for the beef. Although she wanted to slice bigger pieces, she knew the supply had to be stretched so that nobody would leave without something in their belly.

"Thank you." The man was old and dirty, but he smiled and nodded to Savannah. She could see the gratitude in his eyes and wondered when he'd last eaten. He wasn't a regular.

She smiled as she put the slices on a paper plate and passed it to the next person to add a scoop of potatoes.

"You're welcome. Good to see you here."

During a break, the woman who filled the soup cups rubbed her eyes. "Not too busy tonight. Warm outside. People finding some other way to eat."

"I bet it's a lot busier in winter." Savannah had only been volunteering for a few months.

"Hard when we run out of food and there's still a lineup. We do what we can, though."

A woman came to the food line with two small children, and Savannah's heart broke for them. They picked up small bottles of water when they joined the line. What must it be like to have to beg to feed your children? She wished she'd brought some kind of toys to give the kids, but there wasn't much she could do about it now.

First in line was a little girl, maybe eight years old. She had big, wide eyes that seemed to wander all over the place. She likely hadn't seen this much food in one place, at least not recently.

"Thank you," she said politely. "I'm hungry."

"I hope you enjoy it, sweetie."

"I never had beef before."

Savannah kept a smile on her face, but really she wanted to hug the girl.

"I bet you'll love it!"

Next came the girl's brother. He was a couple of years older and Savannah thought maybe he was more used to this. His eyes were glazed over and his mouth a thin line. She put a piece of beef on his plate and said, "Do you like beef?"

The boy moved his head slowly to look at her. For a moment he didn't reply. He licked his lips and locked eyes with her. Savannah felt trapped by his gaze, waiting for him to reply and not wanting to turn away.

Finally he answered. His voice was low and rumbly, like he was being strangled.

"The water is cold."

Savannah froze, the words piercing her like a knife.

"What?"

A agua esta fria.

The boy grinned widely. She could see two missing teeth.

"What did you say?" Her voice was almost a whisper.

"It's cold." He held up the bottle of water he'd picked up earlier in the line. "See?"

He held out the bottle, and she automatically reached to touch it.

"Yes, you're right," she said. "It's cold."

The boy laughed. "I like beef. I like chicken better, but beef is good."

He moved to the next station, and the mother moved into his place.

"So nice of you to help us, dear. I hope God takes care of nice people like you."

Savannah smiled but glanced at the boy as he shuffled along.

Chapter 11
2014

Jeremiah woke and stared at the ceiling above his small bed. It was morning and he hadn't slept much. He'd spent a sleepless night thinking about the girl he watched in the dance studio beneath him.

He'd never felt like this before, and honestly never believed he'd ever have anything close to this reaction to a girl.

"Alannah," he said. He'd whispered her name a dozen or more times through the night, as if he needed to hear the sound of her name to maintain some weird connection with her.

All for nought, though.

He knew there was no chance of anything happening. Compared to him, she was only a little kid. About twenty, probably still a virgin based on how shy she was, probably naïve about the world . . . they'd have little or nothing in common.

But . . .

"But nothing."

He stood and stretched and walked to the window of the living room that looked down to the parking lot of the strip mall. There were only a few cars there this early, but he glanced at all of them, trying to tell himself he was looking for nothing in particular.

She wasn't anywhere to be seen.

He watched for a few more minutes before going for a shower.

While the hot water splashed down on his face, he imagined her being in the shower with him. They would scrub each other's backs, and while he scrubbed hers, she'd look backward to him shyly, with a secret smile. He'd rub her shoulders, neck, and back and then reach around her body to soap her breasts, gently massaging her nipples before kissing her neck as their bodies pressed together. His cock would be pushing against her ass and she'd be arching her body back against it.

He sighed as he continued his fantasy, and his hand found his erection. He rubbed himself, imagining it to be Alannah's hand, imagining them making love in the shower. In his mind, he leaned her against the shower wall and kissed her deeply, then moved down to kiss her tight nipples as the water splashed on them. He kneeled, and his tongue found its way inside her pussy. She moaned, and he felt an animalistic urge to just fuck her. He rose and pressed against her, once again kissing her mouth, and his body reacted as she pulled him even closer to her. He slid inside her, and it was the most amazing lovemaking he'd ever experienced. He pushed slowly, deeper and deeper, and it didn't take very long for him to come. He heard her crying with pleasure as he pushed his cock deep inside her and brought her to her first orgasm.

Jeremiah shuddered as he came himself.

He stood in the shower, the water having turned lukewarm, then cool. He finally noticed and turned the water off and dried himself before getting dressed. He couldn't help but take another look outside the window, but she still wasn't there.

For breakfast, Jeremiah cooked two fried eggs and plopped them onto a slice of toast. He nuked some coffee he'd made the day before to go with it.

"How do you like your eggs, Alannah?" he asked the air.

Twenty-ish *was* too young . . . wasn't it? Almost half his age. Of *course* it was too young. Her skin was smooth and delicate, her cute little body lithe and strong. She wouldn't possibly be interested in him.

With a rush, he pushed back from the table and walked to the bathroom to stare at himself in the mirror. Bloodshot eyes, wrinkles scratching down his cheeks, his hair starting to gray, and some of it falling out.

As much as he tried to keep in shape, he knew he carried twenty pounds more than he should, and if he walked up more than two flights of stairs, he would get winded.

She had the world available to her.

But . . .

When he'd looked into her eyes, he saw a delicate little thing. She was fragile and wouldn't be able to be with just anyone. He understood. He knew from that single meeting that he would be able to take care of her.

She was *nice*. He could tell that as clearly as he could see the red stains in his own eyes. He'd looked into a thousand women's eyes in his lifetime, searching for that one who had the eyes that said, "This is a girl you can trust. She will always treat you well and she's the sweetest thing you've ever met."

Could he really not at least *try* to see if things could work out?

By now, the habit had formed. He walked back to the window and looked out, his heart catching in his chest.

Alannah was standing down below, staring up at him.

* * *

Alannah also hadn't slept well the night before. Part of it was lingering fears from the scary little boy in her mirror, part was the recent note that her twin sister had written in their diary, and part was thinking about the stranger who had watched her dance a few days earlier.

She knew there was nothing to do about the scary little boy. It was just some weird hallucination that she hoped wouldn't recur.

The note from Savannah talked about a different little boy, who scared her at the mission. It was unsettling because Savannah had thought he'd said the same damned words about the water being cold that they'd both heard a couple of times before, but again, Alannah tried to push those thoughts aside.

The stranger who watched her dance, though . . . he was harder to ignore.

He was much older than she, but even so, she felt an instant connection. She'd never believed in love at first sight, but this guy, Jeremiah something-or-other, had her caught in his spell.

Of course she could never say anything to him. He'd laugh and call her a little girl, and she'd feel ridiculous and have to stop going to the dance studio because she'd be too embarrassed to ever see him again.

She could remember his face, the nice smile that lifted the corners of his mouth. His eyes were locked onto hers while they spoke, showing he was actually interested in what she was saying. He seemed like the kind of man who would treat a girl with kindness and respect.

He was gentle but confident. She liked that.

She'd wanted that kind of man without even realizing it.

Of course, maybe he was secretly a hatchet murderer. How could she possibly know any damned thing about him after talking to him once for just a few minutes?

"I just do," she answered herself. "He's—"

She stopped because the next words out of her mouth would have been "The One," and that was too big an image to allow to pass her lips.

He was so much more mature than her, so much more worldly. Surely he could tell her about vast areas of knowledge that she knew nothing about. And she'd love that. His voice was soothing, and she imagined him holding her in his arms and telling her stories he'd lived through. She wondered how it would feel to be held that way . . . .

He was a magician. A *real* magician. That brought emotions of mystery and amazement to her.

Her daydreaming ended as she reached the dance studio.

In front of the shop stood three police officers. One of them stared at her defiantly, arms crossed over his chest. The others were talking to two women. Alannah didn't recognize either of them.

There was a cardboard sign taped to the door of the studio:

CLOSED UNTIL FURTHER NOTICE.

The sign was written in messy blue handwriting that she could barely read.

She stared at the scene, unsure what to do. She wanted to dance, but clearly that was not possible today.

A movement above caught her eye, and she looked up to see Jeremiah staring at her. In that instant, the dance studio fled from her mind, and she focused on him. He was bare-chested, and she blinked, trying to get a clearer view of him.

Then he was gone.

She wished he'd stayed, but his leaving forced Alannah's eyes back to the scene playing out in front of her.

"Nickie?"

With tentative steps, she walked toward the cop who wasn't talking to anybody.

"Hello," she whispered.

She felt scared without knowing why.

He nodded. "Can I help you?" His voice was much gentler than his appearance suggested it would be.

"Is everything okay? Is Nickie all right?"

"Who are you, Miss?"

"I'm Alannah Clark. I take lessons here. Nickie lets me come in whenever I want, to practice. Is she okay?"

"Maybe you should ask her sister."

He pointed to a woman leaning against the wall near the door. She was smoking a cigarette and blowing clouds of smoke.

Alannah nodded.

The sister didn't look much like Nickie. Her face was stretched tightly. Her long, unbrushed hair was ratty.

"Hello?"

The woman stared at Alannah. "What?"

"I'm a friend of Nickie's. Can you tell me what's going on? Is everything okay?"

The sister stared daggers at her, took a long pull on her cigarette, and blew the smoke out slowly.

"She was killed."

Alannah stared for a moment, not wanting to believe what she'd heard.

"WHAT? That's not possible!"

"Somebody strangled her and then stabbed her with a pair of scissors, over and over. Blood everywhere."

"Oh, God . . . I'm so sorry."

"Yeah, well . . ."

"When did it happen?"

"Tuesday."

"I can't believe it. She was so good to me."

"Yeah, well, believe it."

"I'm sorry," she said again.

Alannah stepped backward and wanted to run and hide. She turned around and—

"Whoa!"

—almost crashed into Jeremiah.

"Sorry!"

He'd put his hands on her shoulders to stop her from running into him.

"It's okay, no worries." He nodded his head at the studio. "What happened?"

"Somebody killed Nickie."

"Oh . . ."

They locked eyes and Alannah didn't know what to say. She wanted him to grab her and hug her tightly, but of course he did no such thing. He looked as bewildered as she felt.

She didn't know what to say. She knew she should be crying, losing her mentor and possibly the best friend she'd ever had, but now all she wanted was for Jeremiah to reassure her.

"Can I do anything?" he asked.

She shrugged. She looked into his eyes, and she wanted him to do something, *anything*, but she couldn't find the words.

"I want her back," she said.

He nodded, as if that was the most normal request in the world.

"How about a coffee? I'm not much of a cook, but I do know how to make coffee."

She nodded, and he led her to the door at the side of the studio that led to the stairs.

When they reached his place, he said, "My apartment is like your dance studio. It's where I practice my magic, and the living part is pretty much incidental."

When they walked in to the main room, Alannah marvelled at the shelves and boxes full of gadgets. She saw some large, carefully crafted wooden blocks, lots of shiny steel items, and hundreds of smaller colorful things.

"You have a lot of—" she hesitated and added, "—are they tricks? Is that the right word?"

"Tricks, equipment, articles, things. I'm not much of a wordsmith, but these are the tools of my trade."

"I'd love to see you perform one day."

"I hope that can happen. I'd like that."

He pointed to the far end, "There's my bedroom over there, and the bathroom, and on this side is the place I call the kitchen."

He walked over and started to make a pot of coffee. The area was a side nook off the main room, with a small table and three wooden chairs. There were still crumbs from his morning toast and egg sandwich. He pulled out a chair and gestured for her to sit.

"I can't believe somebody killed her," Alannah said. "Who would do that? She treated me so well."

"I'm sorry. I'll never understand how monsters like that can walk among us."

Tears formed in her eyes as the weight of the loss finally sank in. Nickie had helped her in so many ways, always pointing out the flaws in her dance while praising the perfect flip she might have done or her improvement from a previous attempt. She'd never had anybody to encourage her that way. She barely remembered her mother, and she certainly didn't remember her providing any encouragement on anything. Her father never entered her thoughts at all.

The only person she had in her life was Savannah. Until Nickie.

She wanted to change the subject.

"Tell me about magic."

She smiled and she heard him gasp as she did so.

* * *

Oh my God, he thought. *That smile just nailed me in the chest.*

He didn't know what to say for a moment and bought some time by pouring them each a cup of coffee. She wanted two sugars and he took his black. He took a deep breath as he came back to the table.

"Thank you."

Her voice was tiny, as if she were a Barbie doll. She looked at him with piercing eyes, and at that point he knew the single word that would best describe her: *fragile*.

She was nice and sweet, that he already knew, but she was also so fragile. He wanted to hold her, to protect her and to make sure that nobody ever hurt her for the rest of her life.

He craved her.

And that's just fucking stupid.

But it didn't change how he felt. She kept looking at him, her eyes imploring him to talk, but he couldn't seem to remember how.

Finally he answered. "Magic is the best thing in the world. It allows you to give something to people that they almost never really have. You give them hope. You let them believe that anything is possible, that birds can appear out of thin air and disappear back into it, that people can fly just by wishing it, that we can see into each other's minds and know exactly what we're thinking, and really, we let them believe that dreams can come true."

The corners of her mouth rose and she slowly opened her lips into a huge smile.

"That's so cool. I've never met a real magician. I've seen them on TV, but they can fake anything on TV. It must be so much better in person."

He nodded. "It truly is a joy."

Jeremiah hesitated and took a sip of his coffee.

"I moved here for a reason," he said. "I mean above the dance studio."

She shrugged. "What?"

"I'm looking for an assistant. You know that every magician has an assistant, right? A pretty girl who helps set up the tricks and is always the one the audience watches?"

Alannah nodded.

"The best assistants are very flexible. For some tricks, they need to be able to fit into very small spaces or twist themselves quickly into a certain shape."

She didn't say a word, and Jeremiah knew she was hanging on every word.

"When I watched you dance the other night, I knew you were the one I wanted. You're perfect for me."

"Me?"

He leaned over the table so their faces were only six inches apart.

"You."

She looked down at the table, as if ashamed.

"I'm sorry," he said. "I didn't mean to push."

"No," she blurted out right away. "I'd love that! But—"

"But what?"

"You're not fooling, right? You're not just joking with me? I don't want to . . ." Her voice trailed off, but he heard her finish. Her eyes were closed and a tear fell from one eye. "Please don't tease me."

He reached out with his thumb and wiped the tear away.

"Nothing of the sort. I promise you."

She opened her eyes, and he saw hope. She wanted to believe him.

What happened to you to make you so fragile? he wondered.

"I promise you, I'll take care of you."

Chapter 12
2014

Nickie Amsterdam's funeral was sparsely attended, which surprised Jeremiah. She had been an outgoing woman, she seemed to have a nice personality, and in his dealings with her, she always had a smile on her face.

So, when the entire audience for her funeral consisted of five people, he didn't understand it. Nickie had been his landlord, and he only saw her once a month to pass on the rent check for the apartment above the dance studio. Her sister was there, of course. And he was delighted to see that Alannah was also paying her respects. When she glanced at him and smiled, he made his way over and sat beside her.

"Okay if I join you?"

She nodded.

That left only two other people. One of them seemed familiar, and Jeremiah thought he recognized the darting eyes as belonging to one of the detectives working on Nickie's murder investigation. The other person was a woman who sat several rows back of everyone else. She was older, in her late sixties.

Maybe an aunt or something? he wondered.

The service was held in Foster's Funeral Home, not in a church. Apparently that was Nickie's wish. There were four rows of chairs set out, ten seats in each row, but as 2:00 came and went with no other visitors arriving, a man in his forties walked to the front of the room, turned off the microphone because it clearly wasn't needed, and started to talk about the lasting impression that Nickie Amsterdam left on those she left behind.

The ceremony lasted fifteen minutes. Only Alannah cried. Jeremiah wanted so much to put his arm around her and help comfort her, but that would have been out of line. He did touch her hand at one point, though, and she grabbed it like a drowning woman might grab a life-line. Her hand felt soft and warm in his, and every synapse of his brain seemed to short circuit all at once. He felt lost. He caught his breath and wanted to grab Alannah and kiss her right there.

Instead he found some way to keep his body in check, and eventually he squeezed her hand back.

Jeremiah heard little of the ceremony.

When the man at the front of the room said a last prayer and then silently led the audience down to the back of the room to leave, Alannah finally let go of his hand. He wished the ceremony had gone on for hours.

"I really liked her," Alannah said. "She would let me come in to the studio whenever I wanted to practice. We had formal lessons for two hours each week, and that's all she ever charged me for, but her words and her lessons stayed with me during every practice."

They inched out of the funeral home together. "I can believe that," Jeremiah said. "I liked the few times I dealt with her. She seemed very real."

Alannah just nodded.

He continued, "I can't imagine what kind of a monster could have done this."

She stopped and looked up at him. He hadn't realized before that he was quite a bit taller than her. She was about five foot two, he guessed, so he was a foot taller. She was so cute . . . and once again his mind seemed to short out.

"I know," she said. "She deserved to live a long life."

They walked to the street in silence. He wanted to take her hand again, but he couldn't find the courage. The age difference between them was like a stone barrier.

"Have you thought about my suggestion?" he asked.

For the first time today, she smiled at him.

"I don't really know what a magician's assistant does," she said.

"Oh! Well, how about I buy you a coffee, and I'll tell you all about it."

She nodded. "I'd like that."

* * *

Alannah was by no means sure she wanted to be Jeremiah's assistant. She had thought about it, and although it was true that she didn't know much about what it might mean, she also wasn't unhappy with her current job. On top of that, what about Savannah? They shared the same job and what would she do if Alannah found something else?

That was something best not thought about, at least for now.

But she did like the idea of going for coffee with Jeremiah.

Like? Hell, she would follow this guy anywhere, even though she knew almost nothing about him. It was like he had sprinkled some kind of magical potion on her to entrance her.

He drove them to a nearby Starbucks. She rarely went there so she let him do the ordering. Two grande Caffe Americanos.

They found a small round table in the back. She liked it. It was cozy and intimate. There was music by Taylor Swift playing, quite loudly. Normally she would have complained, but this gave her an excuse to lean closer to him.

"You've never seen a live magic show?" he asked.

She shook her head. It felt like she'd failed a test of some kind.

"Don't worry, it's a lot of fun. I'm the guy that the audience watches the whole time, but it's actually my assistant who does half the work. That's how a lot of the tricks work. They're all watching me, but it's her that's making the magic happen right in front of their eyes. They just don't see what she's doing."

"Like what?"

"Well, some of my favorites are levitation. I'd make you float in thin air. There's two different tricks I like to do that would have you levitating. One of the best tricks, though, is where I would lock you in a cage, cover it with a sheet for a few seconds, and then magically transform you into a tiger."

"What? That's impossible."

She loved the sound of his voice and wanted him to keep talking.

"Nope. It's totally possible. I don't get to perform that one every time I have a show, because I actually do need a real live tiger."

He chuckled and she found herself smiling, looking at his mouth. He had a beautiful smile.

"How would you turn me into a tiger?"

Jeremiah laughed. "You'll have to sign up with me to learn that."

She frowned, but of course that made sense.

"What else?"

"I'll attach you to a large circular board and spin you around while I throw sharp knives at you."

"Umm . . . I'm not sure I like the sound of that one. What if your aim is off?"

"It won't be."

"But what if it is?"

That's when he reached out to take her hand and her life changed immediately.

They looked at each other in silence. She didn't hear the music anymore. She and Jeremiah were locked inside their own dimension, totally apart from the rest of the world.

At that point, she would gladly have let him throw sharp daggers at her. She trusted him more than she'd ever trusted anyone except Savannah.

After a moment when neither of them spoke, he lowered his head to look at their hands.

"I hope that's okay," he said. His voice was soft and whispery, and she thought he was ready to faint if she complained.

"I like it." Her voice was equally tenuous. She gripped his hand tightly. She added, "You're braver than me."

The silence started again as they looked into each other's eyes.

About a million years later, Alannah licked her lips and said, "But what about it? What if your aim *is* off that day?"

He laughed and she basked in the wonderful sound.

"I promise you, you'll never be in the slightest danger."

She nodded, believing him.

"Do you ever do that trick where you cut a woman in half? You must do that, right?"

Jeremiah frowned. "I haven't done that for a long time." He didn't say anything more for a moment, but then he realized he needed to trust this girl and for her to trust him. He did trust her. He didn't really have any reason to do so, but he just did.

That's what it feels like when you meet your soul mate.

"I used to do that trick. It's always very popular with the audience, but I haven't done it in about twenty years. The last time . . . my assistant was badly hurt."

"Oh. What happened?"

"The trick relies on her twisting her body quickly, so her legs curl in above her chest and stomach. It looks impossible from the audience because there isn't a lot of room, but if the box is constructed properly, it's actually quite easy."

He remembered the screams and the blood . . .

"I don't know what happened. I just know that her legs weren't out of the way in time. Maybe she was distracted, or maybe she couldn't get her feet free from the ankle braces in time. I—I really don't know. I just know it was terrible. The saw cut her thighs badly and it took a long time for her to recover."

"Oh my God. That must have been so awful . . . ."

He nodded and forced himself not to let a tear drop from his eye.

Jeremiah reached to Alannah and hugged her.

"I've never told anyone about that before, and here I meet you, you're still practically a stranger, and I'll tell you anything."

She smiled and hugged him back.

"I'm glad you can do that."

After holding each other for a few moments, they slowly separated and sat back down, but this time Alannah reached over to take Jeremiah's hand.

"I'd trust you if you want to bring that trick back to your act."

He stared at her, not knowing how to reply. He hadn't expected to even consider that trick again. Eventually he said, "Thank you. We'll see how it works out."

* * *

An hour later, Jeremiah and Alannah were in his apartment above the dance studio. He showed her some of the magic tricks that he had there, but he could only scratch the surface.

"There's at least a thousand tricks here, mostly small, table magic stuff. Can't do those in my act unless there's a camera and a couple large screens for the audience to see what I'm doing, so I normally only include a few each show. Audiences like the bigger tricks."

"Do you do the thing where you just disappear and then reappear somewhere in the audience?"

"Sure, that's standard."

She walked around the room, seemingly lost in all the gadgets he had there. He watched and enjoyed the look on her face as she glanced among all the items.

After she browsed for a few minutes, he found the courage to do what he'd wanted to do all day. He went to her and put his hands gently on the sides of her face.

She was scared. Vulnerable. He wanted her to be relaxed for this.

"Close your eyes," he whispered.

She did so without question.

He gently kissed her forehead. His lips stayed on her skin for five seconds; he wanted this memory seared into his mind. Then he kissed her all across her forehead, wanting to taste every bit of her.

Each kiss was soft and loving. He kissed her temples and then moved to kiss her eyelids and the space between her eyes. He took his time, cherishing every time his lips touched her.

Her cheeks were next, and her nose. He was forming a map of kisses, and he knew she was enjoying it as much as he was. She didn't move other than tiny bits to have her face press against his lips. He could hear her breathe.

He moved lower, kissing her chin and every square inch around her mouth. Her mouth was open, wanting him to kiss there, but he moved to her neck, while his hands touched her hair. He wanted to kiss her mouth, but he wanted to draw out the tension and suspense. His lips kissed every bit of her neck and then he kissed a path back toward her face, and quietly kissed all around her mouth again.

Finally, he held her cheeks in his hands and his mouth found hers. He kissed her softly, held her there, and then again. His tongue licked her lips slowly, exploring every little bit of them.

Only then did he kiss her slightly more passionately, and that's when she kissed him back.

The kissing went on a very long time.

* * *

He wasn't sure if he led them to the bedroom or if it was Alannah, but one way or the other they ended up sitting on his bed, and he was undoing the buttons on her blouse.

She looked at him, wide-eyed.

"Are you okay?" he asked. He stopped when he saw the uncertainty in her eyes.

She pursed her mouth and nodded.

"It's just that . . . I've never . . ."

She hugged him, not able to finish her sentence.

She's a virgin?

Even though that thought had once crossed his mind, Jeremiah was amazed. She was so pretty, he assumed she'd had lots of boyfriends.

"It's okay," he said as he held her tightly. "I think you'll like it."

He felt her nod, and he kissed her again. She relaxed and allowed him to finish undressing her before he took his own clothes off.

Her body was amazing. As they lay down, he felt every part of her, wanting to know every little bit of her.

She tentatively reciprocated, and she whispered in his ear, "Please be gentle. Please."

Her voice reminded him of the fragility he had sensed in her, and he swore to himself to go slow and be sure she liked everything he did.

Afterward, she was cuddled in his arms and he wanted her there forever. In a ridiculously short time, she had become the most important part of his life, and he would never do anything to let that change.

Chapter 13
2015

And so Alannah became Jeremiah's assistant and his lover.

They spent every minute together, polishing the act and ensuring that everything would go without a hitch.

Alannah was only nervous about one specific trick—where Jeremiah would be throwing daggers at her while she was pinned to a target. That concern lasted until he explained how the trick was done.

"Really?" she asked. "That's it?"

"Yup!"

He had explained that she would be pinned to a target, and he showed her the daggers he would be throwing, which were as real as she had expected.

However, when he threw them, the knives never left his hand. He made the motions to throw them, but then he palmed the knives and slipped them into a secret pocket of his jacket. It looked like he'd thrown them.

Hidden behind the target, which was in front of a curtain, another assistant used a special machine to push a knife in from behind in an instant, making it look like he'd thrown it at her; instead it was punched in from the rear. The spots were carefully selected ahead of time to be close to her body.

It was absolutely safe but looked incredibly dangerous to the audience. They couldn't see the knife fly through the air, but they never questioned that. It just looked like it was going super fast, making the act even more dangerous.

"It's kind of a disappointment to know how it works," she said. "It takes the magic away."

He laughed. "Well, if you want, I can really throw the knives, but . . . ."

"No, that's okay!"

"You're right, magic is only special when you don't know how it's done."

Alannah would be the prime assistant, but there were always a couple of others. Jeremiah usually hired those from a temp agency in whatever city they were performing in. They didn't need to know how the tricks were done, and they left just as puzzled as the audience, but they helped to move things around on stage and they looked pretty, which distracted the audience when Jeremiah was busy doing something he didn't want them to notice. Even so, he always made sure the temp assistants signed a non-disclosure agreement for anything they might happen to see.

The first time Alannah performed with him was in Atlanta. They were booked for a three-night show in a theater attached to a Hilton hotel. The room held five hundred people and all three shows were sold out. That didn't surprise Jeremiah, but it did make Alannah a bit nervous when she first walked onto the stage.

She was dressed in a skin-tight white bodysuit covered with red sparkles. The other assistants wore similar suits but without the sparkles. Alannah's fears soon evaporated when she saw that the audience loved her.

The show went without a hitch, and they did some post-performance celebrations back in their hotel room afterwards.

As they were falling asleep, Jeremiah said, "I've been looking for you my whole life, babe. I can't believe I've finally found you."

"I feel the same way." She nuzzled closer to him and squeezed his arm. "I've never felt so loved and so wanted before."

He kissed her one more time and they gradually fell asleep together.

The world was at peace, and Jeremiah and Alannah couldn't have been happier. The only person who wasn't enjoying their new life was Savannah.

* * *

It was spring and the world was waking up to the sounds of birds chirping. Savannah Clarke was also waking, but she was taking a few moments to stretch and get her bearings. It felt like she'd been sleeping a very long time. She swiveled off the bed and went to the bathroom to splash some water on her face.

The twins were now almost twenty-three, and they'd reached an odd turning point. Up to now, Savannah had called the shots in their lives, but now it seems that was changing. Alannah was the one making the big decisions now, and Savannah didn't like it one little bit.

She brushed her teeth and thought about the soup kitchen. She was expected there at 5:00, and it was only a little after 7:00 a.m. now.

The apartment was quiet. Too quiet. She turned on the radio to hear an ages-old song by Elton John, "Island Girl."

Somewhat suiting, she thought. *I feel like an island these days, cast adrift by my sister, who only cares about that guy.*

She tried to shrug off her feelings.

As always, she went to their shared diary and read Alannah's latest entry.

Who needs Facebook?

Savannah tried not to smile as she read about how happy her twin was, but no matter how hard she tried, she couldn't help but feel happy for her.

She slammed the book shut and put it back without making any notes of her own.

Savannah ate a couple of pieces of toast with peanut butter, and as she munched, she realized she was curious about this Jeremiah guy, and she was going to figure out what the fuss was all about.

After having a shower and getting dressed, she walked outside and felt the glorious sunshine warming her skin. It was already sixty-five degrees and was supposed to go up to eighty later. It felt like it was already there, and she smiled at the trees as she walked, looking at the new buds bursting to life.

She knew where Jeremiah lived, of course. She knew pretty much everything about him. Alannah wrote non-stop in the diary about every little detail. Savannah knew his favorite foods, what he sounded like when he laughed, and every minute of his schedule.

Right now, he would be in his studio apartment, working out details for his next show.

She knew she didn't have to knock. Alannah was welcome there anytime and the door wasn't locked. It'd been years since she'd deliberately impersonated Alannah, but now it was time again.

He was sitting in the living room, and when she entered, a big grin spread across his face.

"Hi! I wasn't expecting you!"

"I missed you. I hope it's okay."

Jeremiah jumped to his feet and moved quickly to her. He gave her a long hug, holding her head close to him, and then he leaned over and kissed her. At first it was a gently soft kiss, and Savannah tried to pretend this was normal, something they did all the time. She kissed him back and then his tongue found hers and the kiss turned more passionate. She reached around him as he did the same to her. Somehow the kiss was still loving and gentle, and she felt lost it in, not wanting it to stop.

He pulled her to him and she felt his erection pressing against her. She pushed herself to it, expecting that's what Alannah would do.

Besides, it felt nice.

Jeremiah broke the kiss and reached around to pull her ass even closer to him.

"God, I want you."

"Me too," she said. And she did.

He led her to the bedroom and smiled as he undressed her and then himself. Savannah stared at his naked body and reached out to touch his chest. She closed her eyes and felt along his body, wanting to know this body that had been making love to her sister

He caressed her in return, while she moved her hands down to his cock. He was rock hard and he gasped when she rubbed him.

"I want to fuck you," she whispered.

She knew Alannah had likely never spoken like that, and she could tell that he liked hearing her talk like that and liked her feeling him like that. She wanted this to be one time he would never forget.

They sat on the bed and then lay down beside each other.

Jeremiah kissed her hard again as she continued to rub his cock and play with his testicles. She knew she was getting wet.

He pushed her to the bed and kissed her neck and breasts. Her nipples were hard, and now she really wanted to feel him insider her.

"Fuck me," she whispered.

He moved over her and she helped guide him inside her.

"God, you feel so good," she said.

He kept on kissing her as he started to push slowly inside her, going deeper and deeper.

Savannah had had sex at least a hundred times, but this was the first time she could call it making love. She felt Jeremiah's emotions and understood why Alannah was so happy. She felt every bit of him inside her and wanted nothing but for it to last forever.

She exploded, and as she did, she moaned and tried not to scream out in ecstasy. She didn't want to scare him. As she came, she pulled him to her and felt him coming as well. He grunted and pushed again. It felt like her orgasm lasted a million years.

When they were finally done, he rolled off and lay beside her.

"Wow," he said. "That was amazing."

"Yes," she agreed. "It sure was. I don't know what came over me . . . ."

"Whatever it was, it can happen anytime. I like that side of you."

Savannah felt a bit of guilt now. "But you like me like I am normally, right?"

He smiled and rubbed her cheek. "I will always love you. Always and forever. No matter what."

She nodded and forced a smile. "Okay. I love you too."

She kissed him again, relishing the feel of their tongues touching.

Chapter 14
2015

The next eight weeks were like a wonderful dream to Jeremiah. He and Alannah worked three cities, and when they weren't performing, they spent a lot of their time together, either practicing or just enjoying each other's company.

They made love often, and over the course of those eight weeks, there were six times when Alannah came out of her shell and treated him to some very special loving. He loved the way she took charge those times and talked dirty to him. She would tell him what positions she wanted and he would follow, ready to try something new.

He never understood what triggered her to be more outgoing, but he also loved how she was most often: quiet, gentle, sensitive, and fragile. He loved how she trusted him to take care of her, and he was always reminded to do exactly that.

"I'll never hurt you," he said often. "Never."

He knew she believed him.

It was hard to find a single waking minute when he wasn't thinking of his dream girl. He was truly blessed to have found the girl he had been looking for his whole life.

It was late May when he made her a simple meal of homemade chili and some toasted garlic bread. They ate at the small table in his studio, and they talked about the weekend show in Newark. Jeremiah hadn't performed there before and was looking forward to it. He hoped he could find some free time to take Alannah to New York City for a bit of a holiday.

"I'd love that," she said when he offered the suggestion.

Her broad smile showed how happy she was with the idea. He saw that smile a lot, and it always made him queasy.

"Oh," he said when they were finished eating. "I have something for you."

"What for?"

"Just because."

He handed her a small unwrapped box. She opened it and plucked out a ring from inside. It was a silver-colored band with a series of small diamonds running along it with smaller diamonds on the edges.

"Oh, I . . . it's beautiful!"

"Do you know what it is?"

She hesitated, looking hopefully at Jeremiah. "I think so—"

He chuckled and got down on one knee.

"My beautiful angel, I've known from the first minute I saw you that I needed to spend my life with you. You've made me happier than I've ever been, and I believe you feel the same way."

She nodded vigorously.

"Will you marry me?"

"Oh my God, yes!"

She fell to the floor alongside him and kissed him over and over and then grabbed him and held him close to her.

Jeremiah could feel her heart beating rapidly. His was doing the same. He closed his eyes and savored holding her.

"We'll always be together," he said.

They silently clutched each other for several minutes before finally separating.

"When do you want to get married?" she asked.

He laughed. "I hadn't thought that far ahead. Do you have any thoughts?"

"Well . . . I'm not really sure. I need to have some time."

"Of course. There's no rush. It'll happen when it happens. If you want a big wedding, that's what we'll have. If you want a small one, that's fine, too. Hell, we'll just elope if that's what you want."

"My head is spinning. I don't know what to say."

"You said 'yes,' which is the only word that matters to me right now."

She smiled. He took her by the hand to the bedroom where they made love again. She was quiet and wanted him to control their lovemaking, and he did everything he could to make it special for her.

* * *

That evening, after they had recovered from the proposal and Alannah headed home, Jeremiah's phone rang.

"Hello?"

"Hi, it's Martin."

Martin Stang was Jeremiah's agent. He worked almost entirely by e-mail, and it was rare for him to pick up the phone and call. Jeremiah couldn't recall the last time they'd actually spoken.

Even the first time they had connected to do business together, it'd been by e-mail. Martin had watched Jeremiah perform in Pontiac, Michigan, at a small night club. He'd only been performing for a couple of years at that point and was still a little clumsy with some of his tricks, but Martin saw the dedication and commitment, and he believed.

"Good to hear from you, Martin. Is this an early Christmas greeting?"

Martin didn't laugh. He was always serious, no matter what, and Jeremiah had never heard him make a joke or send an LOL in an e-mail.

"You won't believe this."

"Okay. Hit me."

"Caesar's Palace called."

"Yeah? They want us back? That's great. They always get the crowds in."

"No, more than that." He paused and Jeremiah decided just to wait him out. There was no point rushing Martin. He'd spill in his own time. "They want to build a new theater. Call it the Jeremiah Moore Theater. Not huge like The Coliseum, of course. Just a thousand seats. Every seat will be a good one. Two shows a night, two-hundred nights per year for ten years.

"What? Slow down."

Jeremiah tried to replay the information in his mind. He felt light-headed and sat down.

"A theater? Just for my show?"

"Yes. And you get to have creative control over the stage design. They want this to be perfect, built to be exactly what you want. After all, you'll be there for a decade."

"If I accept."

"If you accept. Why wouldn't you?"

"What's the money?"

Martin didn't answer immediately. The pause grew longer and longer, and Jeremiah started to get annoyed with his long-time agent.

Finally, he heard the figure. "Ten million a year."

"What?"

"Ten fucking million bucks every year."

Jeremiah didn't know what to say. Now it was his turn to create a long silence.

"You're not shitting me, right?

"Nope. That's the deal."

"Oh my God."

"You'll never get a chance like this again."

"I know."

"Any other questions?"

"How in God's name can they pay that much?"

"Two hundred dates, two shows each night, a thousand seats, a hundred bucks a pop. You can do the math."

"Are there any other conditions?"

"Sure. Pages of them. Nothing you'll care about. It's all legal and timing crap. You have to be there at such-and-such a time every day, every show has to be so long, you indemnify them from any injuries or death you cause, you never speak badly about Caesar's or the show, you do your best to promote the show . . . nothing you haven't seen a thousand times."

"No reason not to agree, right?"

"That's what I figure."

Of course, Jeremiah knew this would be Martin's last and best show, too. He was in his early sixties, and his commission would be $1.5 million per year.

He's earned it, though.

"Let's do it, then!"

* * *

After finishing the call, Jeremiah tried to phone Alannah, but there was no answer. He really wanted to share the good news with her immediately, but no luck. He left her a low-key voicemail message asking her to call him back. He didn't want to spoil it by sounding too excited. He wanted to tell her in person.

He wondered if any magician had ever had a residence show in Vegas, or at least one of that magnitude. He was pretty sure Copperfield had something similar but he didn't know the details.

There were two bottles of Miller Genuine Draft beer in his fridge. He took one and snapped the cap off. He toasted himself and stared out the window overlooking the parking lot.

Before Nickie had been killed, it was possible that Alannah might have been practicing in the studio right beneath him, but that had all come to an end. Nickie's sister had no interest in running the studio, so the doors remained locked. To the best of Jeremiah's knowledge, there'd been no clues found yet as to who the killer was. He assumed the studio was up for sale, but he hadn't seen any signs indicating that.

"Quite a day," he said to the empty room.

It was the best day of his professional life. What he found amazing, though, was that the deal with Caesar's was still only the second best thing to happen that day. Having Alannah say yes to marrying him was better.

* * *

Alannah didn't return his call that night. Or the next day.

Jeremiah was used to there being times when Alannah was hard to get hold of. He wasn't quite sure why, but that would all sort itself out over time. He wasn't always near his phone, either, and he sometimes found himself working long hours designing a new trick, without realizing a whole day might have slipped through his fingers.

He couldn't ask where she was when she was out of touch. It would feel like he didn't trust her. Over time he knew he'd come to learn all of her secrets, and he looked forward to whenever that happened. All he knew was that she wasn't interested in any other men. He knew that as much as he knew his own name. Anything else she might be hiding, he'd find a way to accept.

Finally, she did call, forty-eight hours after he talked to Martin. In that time, the contract had been e-mailed to him (all forty-eight pages) along with Martin's minor suggestions for changes. He read the contract and found it to be more than fair. There was nothing he could suggest to change, and he let Martin know that. He expected the deal to close within a week.

Performances in Vegas would start in six months, on January 2.

When Alannah did call, he was so excited, he almost burst out the news, but he held on, instead asking if she could come over to see him, or alternatively if he could go to her place.

"Oh, you can't see my place. It's too small and I'd be embarrassed."

"Okay."

"But I can be at your place in a half hour!"

"Wonderful! We'll talk a bit, and then I'm going to take you out to whatever restaurant you want. Tonight is a night to celebrate."

And celebrate they did.

Alannah was dressed in a cute, short, light green skirt that showed off her legs. She knew how much Jeremiah liked to see her like that. Her matching top was tight, highlighting the rest of her figure.

When he opened the door, he just stared, marvelling at how beautiful she was.

After a moment, he pulled her into his arms.

"I still can't believe you want to be with me," he said.

"I can't believe *you* want to be with *me*."

For a time, the whole deal with Caesar's was forgotten. He just looked at his amazing girlfriend and felt the love surge through him, as he always did when they'd been apart for more than a few hours.

I can't believe how much love I feel for this girl.

"What's the occasion?" she asked.

He smiled and led her to the couch.

"We need something to toast with." He kissed her lightly on her mouth and then went to open a bottle of sauvignon blanc he'd had chilling in the fridge. He poured two glasses and brought them back, handing her one.

"To our future," he said.

She clinked glasses with him and smiled. They each took a sip, and then Jeremiah blurted out the whole story of the phone call with Martin.

"Your own theater? Like, it won't be used for anything else?"

"That's it."

Alannah's mouth hung open, and he could tell that she didn't know what to say.

"We have our future," he said.

She nodded and her insecurities came to the front. "You're sure you want me to be part of that, right?"

"Oh my God, yes. I need you more than ever."

"Okay. Good. I just needed to hear you say that."

She took another sip and put her glass down. Her face was serious as she stared at Jeremiah.

"I think I need to tell you something."

Chapter 15
2015

The evening that Jeremiah got his life-changing phone call from Martin, Savannah also was feeling that her own life was changing, but not in a good way.

She was lethargic and tired, and part of her just wanted to sleep forever.

Maybe that's exactly what I should do.

The sun had set, and she hadn't bothered to turn any lights on, so the apartment was grim. It was like she was wandering through a forest deep at night. The only illumination came from stray beams of moonlight flashing through the big window in the kitchen, where full moon was rising in the east. The appliances looked like giant gray boulders scattered around her.

She walked to the cutlery drawer and pulled out a carving knife.

Savannah was naked.

She carried the knife to the window. If there had been any light behind her, people below could have seen her from the waist up. She didn't care. All she cared about was being where the light was a little better.

The knife felt as sharp as a razor blade as she ran her finger over it. A tiny stream of blood oozed.

"Wouldn't take much, would it?"

From deep inside her, she could feel distress, but she shook that off. She just didn't care anymore.

The past two months, she had only been happy a few times, mostly the times she fucked

(made love to)

Jeremiah. He treated her unlike anyone had ever treated her. Kindness, gentle touches, always making sure her needs were met . . . she felt alive every second he was touching her body.

But it was all a sham. He wasn't really making love to her, but to her twin sister. How could that go on for long?

Alannah was growing more confident with every passing day. She had decided to quit the job at Millipad so she could be Jeremiah's assistant.

What the fuck?

But as much as Savannah pretended to not understand, she did. Who wouldn't want to be that close to the person who treated you like the queen of the world?

Savannah had no interest in holding the job at Millipad on her own. Half time was hard enough, but no way she'd be able to keep her head straight five days a week with every nutjob in the world calling about problems. She'd go freaking crazy.

That made her laugh. She had enough psychological problems as it was. She had no need for yet another issue.

For twenty-two years, Savannah had been the alpha dog of their tiny pack. Now, she was being pushed to the back while Alannah took control. Alannah, the Angel, was gaining tremendous confidence, while Savannah, the Shit-Disturber, was losing hers.

She wondered if the A and S pendants they'd gotten when they were thirteen were still kicking around somewhere. They had pretty much symbolized their lives since, but she hadn't seen them for years.

She stared out the window. The people below were scurrying to wherever they were headed, some going to visit family, some going to meet a new lover, some just off to a boring job or an AA meeting or whatever the fuck they did with their lives.

Family.

Savannah and Alannah's mom had been dead for six years now. Every time the day rolled around on the calendar, Savannah felt the loss. She wished her mom had been there for her in her growing years. Every July 15, she felt that loss and fought it by remembering how strong she'd been forced to become to compensate for the missing maternal figure in her life.

Today was July 15.

Her mom was in her mind again, but this time there was no offsetting positive factors. She had slid backward in so many ways since Alannah had met Jeremiah.

She ran the knife blade along another finger, opening another thin cut. Blood dripped onto the floor beneath the window.

To kill herself, she'd have to slice the veins in her arms. Lengthwise, not across. She knew how to do it.

The blood on her fingers felt greasy as she rubbed her fingers together. It was dark and looked like oil.

Down below, a man stared up in her direction.

Do you see me?

She stared back at him.

More importantly, do you like what you see?

That thought shocked her a bit. She'd never felt that her body was what she wanted people to crave about her. She wanted them to want *her*.

Didn't she?

She dropped the knife in the sink and went to get dressed.

* * *

An hour later Savannah was standing in a crowded titty bar in downtown Seattle. With it being a Friday night, the place was crowded with men who were looking for a piece of ass.

Interchangeable girls took their turns to prance on stage, smiling fake smiles while taking their clothing off to the music. The mostly drunk men ogled the fake tits and plastic smiles on the stage, stupidly thinking they could fuck the girls if they would just give them half a chance. Maybe giving them twenty bucks would set them apart from the other clowns drooling beside them, so they all eagerly handed over their money, which the girls gladly stuffed into their panties.

Savannah was waiting for a glass of white wine at the bar, while the bartender was busily serving a crowd at the other end.

"Hi," said one guy standing next to her. "What brings you here?"

He was in his mid-twenties, with dark hair and a nice smile. He might have been carrying a few extra pounds, but she didn't care about that.

She smiled back at him. "It was either that or commit suicide."

He laughed. "Well, I think you made the right choice. I'm Dan."

"Savannah. Yes, like the city in Georgia."

Dan laughed again. "Sounds like a sore point."

"Oh, I have lots of sore points."

He nodded and called out, "Hey, Jansen! The lady is waiting for a drink over here!"

The bartender nodded and wound his way over with Savannah's glass of wine.

"Thank you," she said. She wasn't sure herself if she was thanking the bartender or Dan.

"What're the rest of your sore points?"

Savannah thought about all the shit that had been running through her mind earlier. She took a sip of her wine and laughed at herself, which surprised her.

"You know, right now, none of it seems so bad. How about you?"

"I'm doing good, darling. I'm doing very good."

* * *

Savannah finished two glasses of wine before leaving with Dan. He didn't live very close, but he had a car parked nearby, a beat-up, ten-year-old red Chevy. It must have been a nice trophy when it was new, but now it was scratched and dented and stunk of burned oil and cigarettes.

She tried not to care. She also tried not to care that he was drunk and driving.

I was going to kill myself a couple of hours ago, so it'd be stupid to worry about his driving now.

In the bar, Dan had complimented her a lot. She had started to keep a list in her mind for the first hour. Chronologically, he'd told her he liked:

1. Her hair
2. Her smile.
3. Her short skirt
4. Her delicate fingers
5. Her lips
6. Her smile
7. Her boobs
8. Her voice
9. Her laugh

She was pretty sure that he didn't realize he'd duplicated the smile. She also thought he was probably just following some stupid Internet meme about how to pick up girls: just keep telling things you like about them.

The fact is, it worked . . . at least a little bit. He didn't turn to watch the strippers, he didn't seem to be an asshole, and he at least paid lip service to some things he liked about her.

Savannah had done lots worse.

So, she let him take her home, and while he fucked her, she tried to think of being happy. He kissed her all over her body and licked sloppily at her nipples, but he was pretty fast at things and when he entered her, she wasn't wet at all, and it hurt. She squeezed her eyes shut, knowing he could probably have kept on with foreplay for hours and she still wouldn't have gotten excited.

He grunted and came, and she pretended to come too, and he seemed totally satisfied.

"You're awesome," he mumbled. He rolled off her onto his back.

"Back atcha," she said.

He was quiet for a long time, and she wondered if he had fallen asleep.

"I like your eyes," he said.

"Thank you."

After a few more minutes, he started to snore. Savannah climbed out of bed and went to the bathroom to clean up. Then she got dressed and left.

She took a cab home. It was after 2:00 a.m. She went back to the window she'd been looking out earlier and now the street below was totally deserted.

Alannah's bedroom door was shut.

Savannah washed her face and went to her own bed. She cried herself to sleep.

Chapter 16
2015

"I think I need to tell you something."

Alannah immediately shut her mouth, wondering why the hell she'd said that.

Some things were best kept secret, locked in the dark and never bothered. They were grizzly little porcupines that were quiet as long as they were left sleeping, but if you poked them with a sharp stick, you would regret it.

She felt that way now, as Jeremiah looked intently at her, a smile riding on his face and his patience shining through.

How much can I tell him?

She fumbled with her wine and finished the rest of her glass. Then she glanced at the bottle sitting nearby.

"Would you?"

"Of course, sweetie."

Jeremiah poured her another glass, and slid it to her. He held up his own glass.

"To us. To a future that is full of sparkles and magic." He paused and added, "The past can't hurt us. We have our own path in front of us."

They clinked glasses and Alannah smiled.

"Do you have any secrets?" she asked.

He laughed. "I'm sure everyone has secrets. You tell me yours and I'll tell you mine."

"Mine is just kind of weird. It's not really a big deal."

She hoped he would wave it off and say to forget it.

Instead he said, "We shouldn't have any secrets between us. I want us to always trust each other, and that starts by getting rid of any baggage we might have."

She nodded and took a deep breath.

"I've never told you about my family."

She swirled the wine in her glass and stared at it.

"I figured you'd tell me when you were ready."

"My father murdered my mother when I was sixteen. That's when I left home."

"Oh . . . that must have been crazy. Why did he do that?"

"He was just an asshole. I haven't spoken to him since."

"I don't blame you."

He reached out and took her hand.

"And I have a twin sister. She left home with me."

"A twin? Identical or fraternal?"

"Identical."

"Where does she live? In Seattle?"

"Yes, we actually live together. She's not big on meeting people, though. One day you'll meet her."

He shrugged. "Okay. Is that your secret?"

"Part of it. But, your turn. What's *yours*?"

Jeremiah leaned back and his smile disappeared for a moment before reappearing.

"I have a terrible temper. It's one of the worst parts about me, and I wish it wasn't true, but it is."

"Really? I've never seen you even a little irritated, let alone lose your temper. That's almost funny to hear you say that!"

"Well, it's not funny when it happens. I've mostly been able to control it since I was a teen, but back then, it was really pretty bad. I was always in fist fights with friends, and I often lost my temper with my little brother. I hated that. It's like I would totally lose control of who I was, and my body would go on this rampage."

He stopped, apparently thinking back.

"I hated when that would happen. I'm glad I can mostly keep that temper under control, but it's still there. If something gets me mad—like, really mad—I feel that loss of control coming on, and I know one day I might explode and lose myself like I used to."

Alannah didn't say anything, just nodded. She felt a chill so she went to the kitchen area and put her sweater on her shoulders.

"That's your only secret?" she asked. She wanted something bigger, something that would be more equal to her own secrets.

"That's it. You already know about the other big thing in my life, when I cut that girl who was my assistant."

They sat in silence for a moment, holding hands and looking into each other's eyes.

"You're my dream girl, you know," he said. "I will always love you. Always and forever."

"Always and forever."

"Do you want to tell me the rest?"

She nodded.

Only part, she decided.

"Sometimes I'm haunted by a little boy."

Jeremiah pulled his hand away.

"What do you mean?"

"He speaks Portuguese and started to show up years ago, saying 'The water is cold.' I didn't know what he is talking about. Sometimes when I look in the mirror, his face stares back at me. He's dead, I think."

"That's—"

"Crazy?"

"No, I didn't mean that."

"It's okay. I know it's crazy, but it's true. A couple of times he's said things in English, too. Something about coming back."

"That must be so scary."

"It is. Especially when it's in the middle of the night, like if I wake up and have to go pee and glance at the mirror. It's really, really scary."

"Oh, God, I hate that thought."

He moved to her and held her tightly to him.

In the background, Alannah could hear light rain outside, and she wondered if the dead boy was hiding between the raindrops.

"Alannah?"

"Yes?"

"Did something happen to you? Sometimes you seem frightened, like you want to hide from the world. I love those times, because I just want to take care of you forever. But, I've wondered how you got to be the person you are."

Alannah pulled back from him.

"I don't know what you mean."

"You're like a china doll, and I worry that you might break. I never want to do that accidentally, and if I knew more—"

"There's nothing to know," she snapped.

He nodded. "Okay."

Alannah walked away and crossed her arms. "I've told you everything."

"Okay," he said again. "I'm sorry."

He went to her but she looked at her watch. "I should head home. It's late."

She didn't want to leave this way, but she knew she had to.

She kissed Jeremiah good-bye, leaving him to wonder what the hell had just happened.

* * *

The air outside was warm, and Alannah didn't really need to wear her sweater, but she liked the coziness on her arms. She walked away from Jeremiah's apartment but didn't head home. She wanted to be alone and walk.

After thirty minutes of distracted meanderings, she realized she wasn't completely sure where she was. Seattle had lots of twisting streets and she had just followed her feet. She found herself in an empty park and sat on a bench.

In front of her was a baseball diamond. She imagined teams had been playing there earlier, but now it was close to midnight and only a handful of teenagers walked together in the middle of the outfield. They smoked, and she suspected the cigarettes weren't of the legal kind. She didn't care.

The moon was high above her, almost full, and it cast hard shadows from the trees near her.

Alannah hated how she'd left Jeremiah. He was the only man who'd ever treated her well, and for some reason she'd gotten into a huff and, well, hopefully she could smooth it all over tomorrow.

"I'm coming back."

The voice came from behind her, and she felt her hair stand on end. It was *right* behind her.

She didn't move. Maybe it would just go away if she pretended not to notice.

One of the teenagers in the field laughed. They were too far away to help her if she needed help.

The wine had made her feel slightly buzzed earlier, but right now she was stone sober and scared out of her mind. She willed the dead boy to leave her alone.

Nothing happened. She shut her eyes and tried to hide inside herself, and after a few minutes, she wondered if she had imagined the voice, because it hadn't happened again.

Then she felt breath on the back of her neck. She heard someone breathing, and hot, sticky exhalations dotted her neck.

Oh, please go away, she willed. She still didn't move.

The second time he spoke, his voice was right by her ear.

"I'm coming back. And I'm going to kill him."

She screamed and ran, not looking back to see the dead boy laughing at her.

Chapter 17
2015

Jeremiah couldn't sleep that night. He wanted to kick himself for pushing Alannah about whatever secrets she might be keeping to herself. She needed to tell him in her own way, at her own pace. He knew she was gentle and sweet and easily hurt, but he'd gone ahead and pushed anyhow.

That morning he called to apologize. She made it sound like it was no big deal, but he knew better. He vowed to never do that again.

Unless I lose my temper.

It was always there, just below the surface, the fear that somebody would say the wrong thing and he would blow. He remembered losing his temper completely, the time he tossed his little brother's games down the stairs. And the time he had killed the cat.

That must never ever happen with Alannah.

She was sensitive, so very sensitive, and he knew if he lost his temper, he'd also lose her. Probably forever. And he would deserve it. He simply couldn't let that happen, no matter what.

In his e-mail that morning, he had received a general schematic of the new theater from the design team at Caesar's. He printed the fifteen-page PDF and spent an hour poring through the details. In the end, he didn't have much to suggest. They'd included several trap doors in the stage that would be invisible to the audience and a couple of catwalks running from the stage into the audience, so he could greet more people.

They had also planned equipment to allow him or his assistants to fly above the crowd, held up by nearly invisible wiring. The one addition he wanted to include related to that. He wanted the assistants to start the show by flying from the back of the theater to the stage. He'd seen that done by Cirque du Soleil once, and it had caught everyone off guard. He wanted that effect.

He didn't have much to say about the seating. The areas up close would be arranged as a dinner theater, with round tables of eight seats each. Each seat would cost $200, which included a basic dinner. Booze was extra, of course. *A lot* extra.

The rest of the theater used standard stadium seating so there would be no bad seats anywhere—no seats blocked by pillars or anything else.

The plans were amazing, and he had to keep himself from shaking his head and convincing himself it was all just a dream.

* * *

Construction of the new theater began almost immediately after the contracts were signed. Jeremiah visited the site monthly to check on progress and was amazed at how fast it developed.

There were no indications on the site as to what the new theater would be used for. Caesar's wanted to surprise everyone when everything was in place.

He loved it.

Although he performed a few shows while waiting for his theater to be complete, he instructed his agent not to book anything new. Jeremiah wanted the time free to plan the new spectacle.

Alannah helped with organizing. She set up a system on her iPad that kept track of the thirty standard tricks he would perform for any given show. Some of them were "small" magic, work that needed a camera to show the audience what was going on. He only included his favorite card tricks and mind-reading. These always went over well, but the audience didn't go to see him for those.

They wanted the big shots.

They wanted levitation, disappearing girls, danger, thrills, and surprises.

They wanted to *believe*.

Alannah kept track of the major tricks in her iPad, along with substitutions. Jeremiah didn't want to perform the same set of tricks every night, although he was known for a few spectacular ones that he would repeat over and over, so the audience didn't feel cheated.

However, there were a half dozen different levitation tricks and several ways to make his assistant disappear; on top that, in addition, he had way too many tricks in his bag to perform them all. If he tried to include every trick he knew, his show would last all night long.

One thing nagged at him as they planned.

Every time he had ever asked his audiences for feedback, they always overwhelmingly responded by asking about the one trick missing from his act: cutting a girl in half.

The contract with Caesar's had an appendix that listed eight major tricks that he was obligated to perform in each show. After all, they were putting up a shitload of money to build the stage, and they needed the audiences to come.

Number three on that list was cutting a girl in half.

Jeremiah knew that, of course, and now he was committed. It was time to bury the past.

* * *

On December 10, Jeremiah and Alannah boarded an Alaska Airlines flight for Las Vegas, three weeks before the first show, but there had been little point going earlier because the stage hadn't been finished. Now, they could practice all they wanted with no fear of construction workers interrupting them.

The Jeremiah Moore Stage. It still sounded surreal to them.

The plane was a 737, three seats on each side with an aisle down the middle. Alannah took the window seat and Jeremiah the middle. The aisle seat was empty, which they were both happy with.

The flight was only two hours and fifteen minutes, and as they lifted into the air, Alannah leaned over to kiss Jeremiah and said, "Onward to our new life."

"Yes. I can't wait to get it started!"

She grabbed his arm when the plane rumbled through a spot of turbulence. She wasn't afraid of flying, not exactly, but she felt the adrenaline flooding her when things got a little bumpy.

He'd hired three additional assistants from the local temp agency. Although he hadn't met them yet, he'd interviewed them on Skype, and they seemed to be good fits. Really all they needed was to seem excited to be part of the show and be attractive and reliable. If any of the three impressed him over the first month, he'd hire her full time. This was a long gig.

"Are you going to miss Seattle?" he asked.

"No, I don't think so. It's been my home for a long time, now, but it's not like I have any actual roots there. I grew up in a small town in upstate New York. Even there, I didn't feel any loss when we left. I just needed to leave.

"Here, I don't feel the need to leave. I'm moving on with you, and there's nothing that could make me happier."

"I'm glad."

She smiled broadly for him.

"And you're sure your sister really wants to move, too?"

"Yup. She'll come a bit later, but she would never live in a different place from me."

"I still have to meet her."

Alannah leaned onto his arm. "You will. It's a bit complicated right now, so don't worry."

Jeremiah wanted to ask what was complicated, but he knew she'd tell him when she was ready.

"You know, Vegas is known for a lot of things," he said. "Music, the shows, of course, gambling, the heat."

"Yes. I'm looking forward to seeing it all!"

"And one other thing."

"What?"

"Weddings."

"Oh, like that chapel where somebody dressed as Elvis Presley can marry people?"

"That, and of course slightly more respectable places."

"I guess."

"How would you feel about us getting married? I mean, now, not some indeterminate point in the future, but . . . well, now?"

She turned and stared at him.

"Really?"

"Yes, really."

She pursed her lips and kissed his cheek.

"That would be amazing . . . to be married to you right away. I'd love that . . . ."

"But?"

"It's just . . . complicated. I'm not sure I can do it that fast."

"Oh, okay."

Jeremiah looked into her eyes and tried to hide the sadness that rushed through him. He wanted this girl to be joined to his heart forever. Not that a cheap ceremony would change anything if their relationship went sour, but the symbol felt important to him.

"Soon," she whispered. "I promise."

She grabbed his thigh and squeezed it. He tried to believe that everything would be perfect for them.

It has to be, he knew.

* * *

The plane landed five minutes ahead of schedule and they found their way through the labyrinthine terminal, grabbed their bags, and hired a taxi.

"Caesar's Palace," Jeremiah told the driver.

"Sure thing."

The cabbie stared at him using the rear-view mirror, possibly trying to figure out if he was a big tipper. Or maybe trying to see how a guy his age had somehow attracted a beautiful girl half his age.

Surely that's not unusual in Vegas, thought Jeremiah. *And who gives a shit anyway?*

The hotel expected them. As they climbed out of the cab and paid the driver, a woman walked out and said, "Mr. Moore. Ms. Clarke. My name is Amanda Smythe, and I'll be responsible for getting you both settled today."

They said "Hi" at the same time and shook hands. The woman looked to be about fifty with short curly gray hair. She wore a tan, knee-length dress that must have been hot, but she didn't show it.

"Your rooms are ready. You have connecting suites on the twentieth floor. I trust they will be appropriate until you find permanent arrangements."

She smiled at Alannah and nodded at Jeremiah.

"Well, that'll come with time," he answered.

"Of course."

She called to a bellboy and told him to take their luggage to their rooms.

"I'm sure you'd like to see the theater first," she said.

"You bet."

She walked them through the tourists that flooded the main floor. The farther they walked, the more slot machines surrounded them, and the more people crowded around them. None of them recognized Jeremiah, but he hadn't expected them to.

It was only two o'clock in the afternoon, but the casino was packed. Several times they had to detour around intoxicated guests.

Jeremiah had performed in Las Vegas at least a dozen times, but only once at Caesar's Palace, about five years earlier. He wasn't fazed at all by the crowds, the drinks, the noise, the gambling, but he could tell that Alannah was soaking it all in, never having seen anything like this before.

There's no place in the world like Vegas. He promised himself to find time over the next month to show her the wonders of the city.

Even a month would only make a small dent in the sights to be seen, but it was a start.

We have our entire lives to appreciate the rest.

And then, they were there.

Their walk ended in a hallway with a sign above the entrance, but it was draped so nobody could read it.

"Here is the entrance to your stage," said Amanda Smythe.

They stopped and Jeremiah felt his heart beating. It was one thing to see blueprints but quite another to see that somebody had invested millions of dollars to build a stage just for him.

The walkway was blocked by two security guards, but they didn't budge when the trio walked past. The walkway was at least fifteen feet wide and snaked in a curving pattern. The walls were mirrored, as was the ceiling. There was no obvious lighting, but there was enough ambient light somehow.

Sound filtered from all around them, dark moody music, perfect for magic.

"Oh God, this is amazing," said Alannah.

"I know," he answered. "I can't believe it."

They walked slowly, dazzled by the mirrors, and noticed that the mirrors had shadows that appeared every once in a while. Shadows of magic being performed. They only appeared for a second, just long enough to register and make them wonder if they'd really seen anything.

After a few minutes, they entered an atrium with a half dozen doors that looked like they guarded an ancient dungeon: oak, heavy, scratched, like they'd seen a thousand wars.

"The lighting will be up, so you can inspect anything you wish, but of course that's way brighter than it will normally appear."

They both nodded, both speechless.

The dungeon-like doors swung open and they went inside.

Chapter 18
2016

It was January 1, and Alannah was feeling nothing but butterflies. The first show was tomorrow, and although they'd practiced and practiced, it was still a huge event, and she was close to freaking out.

She was sitting behind the stage, trying to calm herself. Jeremiah was out front, talking to the lighting director. This was the last full dress rehearsal before the real thing, and they wanted everything to be perfect.

Alannah had messed up a couple of times when Jeremiah magically transformed her into a tiger. That was the trick she was most worried about.

The rehearsal started at 10:00 a.m. Alannah and the three temp assistants got into place at the back of the theater. They climbed some hidden ladders and waited.

Deep baritone music fill the theater. The acoustics were perfect; Alannah could hear every note clearly and there were no echoes. The music rose in pitch and volume, and the lights in the theater went out when the sound reached its climax. The sound stopped as suddenly as the lights, and she imagined the audience, shocked by the sudden transition to darkened silence.

A moment later, the first pyrotechnics showered the stage. When the glare dissipated, the spot lights engaged, focused on Jeremiah at center-stage.

He waved his arms, and Alannah and the assistants started to fly down toward him. The wires holding them were completely invisible and, when they landed on the stage, disengaged without being touched. The four woman looked like magic elves appearing from nowhere.

Jeremiah wanted to start the show with a bang…by turning Alannah into a tiger. Once she got past that act, she would relax.

Jeremiah had always planned for the music and other background noise to be an integral part of the show, along with the fireworks and lighting. Every piece of the puzzle had to fit together perfectly.

He held his arms out as if commanding attention and directed a large cage to be rolled out. The cage had solid steel bars, and the back was draped with a large cape.

Jeremiah helped Alannah enter the cage while the other assistants danced around. Fireworks blasted off almost at random, keeping the nonexistent audience captured.

When Allannah was in the cage, Jeremiah pulled the cape all the way around, so that nobody could see inside. He gestured for the cage to be lifted into the air, so the audience would see that there was no way for Alannah to escape.

She knew that from their perspective, she would be transformed into a tiger, and it would seem astonishing.

The audience would start the process of wanting to believe. That's what Jeremiah needed.

In reality, though, the trick wasn't the slightest bit magical. She knew (but the audience didn't) that the back of the cage was faked. It looked like the same steel bars that the rest of the cage was made of but was instead a thin wooden wall painted to look real. Behind the wall the tiger was waiting. Moments before, his trainers had settled him in the cage, bribing him with pieces of raw meat, and then lifted the fake cage backing.

As soon as the cape hid what she was doing, Alannah pulled a small trap door in the bottom of the cage and slid into the tight area beneath. It was the kind of trick that needed a slim assistant to work. From the audience's perspective, there didn't seem like anywhere near enough room for somebody to hide. That was the secret of most tricks in which the assistant disappeared.

She hurried into her hidey hole and pulled a cord that released the fake wall. It crashed to the floor, on top of her and the rest of the cage. The tiger was free.

The sound of the wall crashing down was hidden by the loud music and fireworks that Jeremiah used to distract the audience. He would hear it, though.

A few seconds later, he'd pull the cape off with a big flourish, and the transformation would be complete.

Alannah was now a tiger.

It worked like clockwork.

The cage was taken off the stage and the handlers took care of the tiger, allowing Alannah to be freed.

She punched the air with both arms, loving how well the trick worked. She couldn't wait to hear the audience's reaction tomorrow night.

Still off stage, Alannah dropped into a tunnel and waited for her cue to climb onto the middle of the stage. This time she was hidden only by darkness, as Jeremiah stood to one side with the spot light on him. The darkness only lasted a few seconds, and she climbed up exactly as planned, magically appearing out of thin air.

She smiled. The show was going to be great.

The rest of the rehearsal went without the slightest problem, and they were ready.

Thirty minutes later, after a quick debrief, Alannah wanted to be alone. The excitement had given her a headache, so she went to her dressing room behind the stage and sat on the floor, leaning in a corner of the small room.

A sudden sleepiness come over her, draping her like the cover in the tiger cage. Her eyes closed almost on their own, and she fell asleep within a minute.

* * *

The next couple of hours were quiet in the Jeremiah Moore Theater. Most of the staff had left to be with their families on New Year's Day. Only a few holdouts still hung around, mostly people who didn't have any family to go home to.

This was the first time that Savannah Clark had seen the inside of the theater. She had read detailed descriptions of it from Alannah's diary, of course, but nothing really prepared her for the glitziness, the size, the amazing technical triumphs that allowed people to fly and invisible trap doors to swallow people. Even though she knew the trap doors were there, when she bent down and tried to find them on the stage, she couldn't. The floor was beautiful hardwood and looked better than the living room of any house she'd ever seen.

She walked through the seating area, trying out various chairs, and every one was perfect.

The back of the theater opened out to the waiting area that connected to the main part of Caesar's by the snaking mirrored walkway.

She went to that walkway and couldn't help herself. She laid on the floor and looked at the ceiling. Her image looked down at her, and she laughed. It was surreal to see herself hanging in the sky with no support.

"Nice, isn't it?"

A man stared at her from the doorway to the theater.

"It sure is," she said.

"I'm Will. One of the electricians." He moved toward her.

"Savannah. I'm nobody, I guess."

He grinned. "Can't say I agree with you there."

He locked eyes with her and stepped closer. His eyes wandered down her body.

"You don't work here?" he asked.

"Does it matter?"

What the hell?

She moved to him and didn't hesitate. She took his face in her hands and kissed him.

He kissed her back hard, greedily, as if it'd been a long time since he'd been with a girl. He was hungry for her body.

Savannah didn't mind. It'd been a long time for her, too. She thought to the last time she'd pretended to be Alannah with Jeremiah. A month ago? Six weeks? Either way, she was overdue.

Will's hands roamed over her body, and she felt every touch.

She whispered in his ear, "Over here. It's secluded enough."

She led him to the main part of the theater, near the back. It wasn't dark but neither was it lit as brightly as other areas.

Everyone's left, anyhow.

She kissed him again, passionately, their tongues meeting and playing. His erection was pushing against his jeans, and she undid his belt, unzipped him, and pulled his pants to his ankles. She wanted this to be something he would remember.

She heard a couple of small noises from farther down the stage, but they barely registered on her. She was totally preoccupied.

Savannah knelt and took his cock into her mouth. She pushed it in as far as she could without choking and clamped down on it. She knew the warmth of her mouth would make him go crazy. He held her head with his hands as she bobbed up and down, his balls in her hands.

"Oh God," he moaned. He braced himself and pushed her head gently in the rhythm she was setting, and it didn't take very long for him to come.

He moaned louder and pushed her head down.

She swallowed what she could and licked his cock, slowly removing herself from it.

"Next time, it'll be my turn," she smiled as she stood up.

He just nodded.

As he reached down to pull his jeans up, Savannah could see over his shoulder. Jeremiah Moore had been watching the entire time. He stared in horror, then turned and ran from the theater.

Chapter 19
2016

Amanda Smythe had watched a number of the rehearsals and now that it was officially Day One, she was a nervous wreck. She could only imagine how Jeremiah and his team were feeling.

Amanda had met the magician and his fiancée when they arrived at Caesar's Palace and she'd shown them around the digs, but there was a lot she didn't tell them.

She didn't tell them that it was her idea in the first place to build the theater and offer Jeremiah the ten-year contract. She'd put together the figures, verified them with her best contractors, co-ordinated customer surveys asking what they'd think of a world-class magic show being stationed at Caesar's, and most importantly, convinced the Board.

She remembered the presentations she'd put together, the arguments from the nay-sayers, the eventual agreement (because, really, how can you argue with the bottom line figures she'd come up with?), and finally working with the legal team on Jeremiah's contract.

Amanda didn't want Jeremiah and Alannah to know that the theater wouldn't exist if she hadn't imagined it into being. She knew that would make them look differently at her, and she just wanted them to see her as some kind of co-ordinator.

It was 8:00 p.m.

Curtain time.

She sat in the back, because that would give her the best perspective of the entire show. The house was filled, as she had predicted. In fact, the first night had sold out within two hours of the official press release. Everyone important had to be there at the premiere, which is why the ticket prices were doubled for tonight.

The best table had seating for eight, and she'd sold it for $50,000. Now she looked over to see Robert De Niro sitting with his wife and six people she didn't recognize. He would have paid double the price for the table.

Amanda couldn't eat. She knew in her heart that everything was going to run like clockwork, but there was so much riding on it. If the first year went as planned, with mostly sold-out shows each night, she'd look like a genius and that vice-presidency she'd dreamed of for the past year would be locked in.

If things didn't go so well . . . well, there was no point thinking of that. It wasn't going to happen.

Try telling my stomach that.

The music rose and the show started.

The audience loved the assistants flying above their heads to join Jeremiah at the stage. First check mark!

Amanda tried to relax as the waitress placed a martini on her table. She took a drink and a deep breath to go along with it.

Just enjoy the show.

She was sitting in a crowd of strangers. None of them knew her and she knew none of them. Exactly how she wanted it.

When Alannah was transformed into a tiger, the audience gasp. Amanda smiled, finally feeling a little bit at ease.

The members of the Board would be watching the show on closed circuit TV. She'd invited them all to attend the show in person, but none of them took her up on her invitation. That was fine with her.

The feeling in the room was amazing. She loved the tension, the dread when a dangerous trick was performed, the thrills . . . the magic.

The audience *loved* the magic.

So did she. She almost felt a tear forming in her eye, but it didn't get far enough to drop. She wasn't built that way.

On the stage, they were setting up for the last big, dangerous trick: cutting the girl in half.

More fireworks sprayed from the stage as the box was wheeled on stage. The box reminded Amanda of a casket. Jeremiah spun it around several times and opened it so everyone could see it looked like just a plain old box, the kind a girl would have no way of escaping from.

"And now!" yelled Jeremiah from the stage. His voice was amplified by a tiny microphone hidden behind his left ear.

He helped Alannah climb in.

Just for a moment, Amanda thought she saw something on his face. An unusual look as he locked eyes with Alannah just before enclosing her.

Amanda had watched this trick several times. There was something different this time. She leaned forward trying to figure out what was going on.

Alannah's head was sticking out one end of the casket. The audience knew that her feet were shackled at the other end with no way for them to be freed.

Of course, in reality, Alannah could easily get her feet out of the shackles because her ankles were much slimmer than anyone would have expected. She had done it fifty times with no problem.

This time, though, it looked like real fear on her face. She looked up at Jeremiah, and Amanda was sure she saw her mouth form the word, "Please."

The casket was made of heavy oak.

Jeremiah spun it around so that everyone could see that the girl was indeed trapped. This is when Alannah should have been moving her legs up to her chest.

Most magic acts use a simple lumberjack's saw to cut through the box. What other magicians use had never been good enough for Jeremiah Moore. That was why he was considered the best in the business.

Lowering from the ceiling was a giant circular blade, four feet in diameter. When it was near enough, Jeremiah plucked some of the blades to show it was solid steel. And it truly was.

The blade started spinning.

"No," whispered Amanda. "It isn't right."

She still didn't know what was wrong, but her senses were heightened after seeing how Jeremiah and Alannah had looked at each other. It was a look that said, "Good-bye."

He nodded, and the saw began to spin.

She wanted to jump up and stop the show, but of course that would be her own ruin. She needed this show to be a success.

Jeremiah explained to the audience that the blade was spinning at 2,400 revolutions per minute.

Alannah was calling from the box in distress.

That was part of the act. She'd done the same thing every time Amanda had seen a rehearsal.

But is it the same? She's calling much more loudly.

Jeremiah waved to some hidden facilitators, asking them to lower the blade.

The audience was on edge. Even though many of them had seen this trick on television, it was much edgier to see it up close and personal.

Alannah screamed louder. "HELP ME!"

The blade dropped and started to dip below the edge of the casket.

Alannah's screams cut off, and suddenly the blade was red.

Amanda stared as if the whole thing was happening in slow motion. The entire blade was crimson, seemingly all at once. Then blood spurted in all directions from the box.

Alannah moaned and fell silent.

The blade kept lowering, as it was programmed to do, until it was at the bottom of the box.

Jeremiah did not move. Amanda thought he must have been in shock.

Then, the theater lights went out and stayed out for five minutes.

At first the audience gasped and whispered, thinking this was part of the show, but it quickly became apparent that this was not planned.

Robert De Niro had blood splattered on his shirt. As soon as the lights came up, he motioned to his group to move away.

Alannah's head was no longer sticking out of the box. The cascade of blood covering the floor and the box made it clear she must be dead.

But her body was gone.

Part 3

The Big Reveal

"Magicians will always tell you the trick is the most important
thing, but I'm more interested in telling a story."

—Marco Tempest

Chapter 20
2018

Brian James Clark woke on day 9,490 of his incarceration. He knew the number of days exactly because there was little else for him to do in his cell other than count the days, even the hours. It was that number of days since he'd killed the tramp he'd been married to, and he still didn't regret it one little bit.

The justice system pretended to want to rehabilitate him. What a joke. He'd played by the rules all of his life until Marianne took him for a fool and ran around, sleeping with every guy she could find. Killing her was the best decision he'd ever made.

Since his arrest, he'd been in various cells. First the local jail, then the holding pen near Syracuse, New York, and after his life sentence, he'd lived in three different 8 x 10 foot cells in the Otalay Prison in New Jersey. He didn't mind it, since he got three squares a day, all the reading material he wanted, and bits and pieces of courses that helped him learn how to use his mind. And, of course, he had lots of company.

His field of study was science, in particular, cosmology and quantum mechanics. If anyone had asked him what either of those terms meant before his prison term, he'd have stared at them with no comprehension at all.

Things change, though. Everything in his life had changed except for his feelings about his cunt of a wife, Marianne.

Brian was the prisoner who'd been in Otalay the longest, and he took that with a bit of pride. Why not?

In the twenty-six years he'd lived there, he'd had no visitors other than his lawyer, who came by every five years or so to let him know he wasn't completely forgotten.

"Just waiting for the next parole date," the scumbag always said.

"Whatever."

Brian was now fifty. He was puzzled by his lawyer talking about parole. What the heck would he do if that ever happened? He had no way to make a living, no place to stay, no family, no friends on the outside. How in God's name would he be better off out there? It'd just be a fucking mess.

Otalay was home.

No family.

That's not completely true, he supposed, but it might as well have been. No visitations in 9,490 days sure the fuck sounded like no family to him.

He shrugged and stood to stretch his legs. It was almost exercise time.

He did miss women, though. He missed hearing their voices, touching them, making love to them. Sometimes he wondered if that was only a theoretical feeling, though. How would he react if a woman actually came to see him for some reason? Would he end up wanting to fuck her, like he expected he would, or would he just find her a boring twat who should leave him alone.

These were the kinds of questions Brian Clark thought about sometimes, in between reading about the quantum foam and string theory.

He never thought of Alannah or Savannah. It'd likely been at least a decade since either of those names trickled through his mind.

Marianne did sometimes come to him. Sometimes in the middle of the night, he'd awaken with a hard-on, remembering how she'd suck his cock. He liked that.

When that happened, he'd rub one out and then roll over and go back to sleep. She's visited less and less, but he hadn't noticed.

The prison stank of sweat. Most of the inmates stank, and Brian knew he did, too, but he didn't care more than anyone else did.

The smell sometimes made him remember he was still alive. *That couldn't be bad.*

He was frail, thin, and would likely lose in a fistfight with a thirteen-year-old boy, but he was still alive.

More importantly, he still had a role to play.

He just wasn't sure yet what that role was.

Chapter 21
2018

Jeremiah Moore sat underneath an old pine tree, his back against the trunk. He was forty-two and felt every minute of those years. Every muscle was sore.

He wore a St. Louis Cardinals baseball cap and a matching jacket. It was September, and the Cardinals weren't in contention. Neither was he a fan. He just felt that he needed camouflage to blend in, not wanting anyone to recognize him.

He spent his days as an unskilled laborer, loading and unloading cargo from freight trains. Whenever he had a choice, he worked the midnight shift, because there was even less of a chance of running into anybody who might recognize him.

Before the fiasco at Caesar's Palace, he'd been on television dozens of times, everything from Jimmy Fallon to the worst of the daytime talk shows. He'd needed to get his act in front of the American people, and now he wished they'd just all forget who he was.

For the first few months after the accident, he lived in Las Vegas, but with the story in the national headlines every day, it soon became too difficult. Not only had he lost Alannah, he'd lost pretty much everything that he cared about.

The show was cancelled, of course. He didn't complete even a single night of the ten-year run.

The magic was gone. Nobody would ever ask him to perform again, and he didn't blame them one little bit.

His ability to grieve in private was gone, too, because everywhere he went, people stared at him. He was the freak of the week on every news broadcast, and the city of a million tourists appointed him the newest kick-me kid.

Caesar's sued him for the cost of building the theater plus lost income plus legal costs. He didn't contest. It wouldn't matter because he'd lost every penny and had no way to use his talents to earn more.

Not that he would have.

Magic was dead.

More importantly, though, by far the worst part of the whole ordeal, was the loss of Alannah.

He still loved her, even though he knew what had really happened. He still had no clue why, but he would forgive her anything.

Always and forever.

He'd always told her he'd love her always and forever. "Always" meant there would never be a single second that he didn't. "Forever" meant it would extend into the future as long as he lived.

And he still did love her. If it was possible, he loved her more today than when the murdering saw cut through the box she was trapped in and the blood came gushing out.

He knew it made no sense, but it was true. She was his soul mate, and he would give anything to have her back.

"Alannah, I miss you."

He whispered the words under the pine tree as he lay down his iPad. He'd just spent an hour reading the final report of the investigation. How it could have taken two years was totally beyond him, but the official Crime Scene Investigation into "Incident 2016-10320-2 at Caesar's Palace, Jeremiah Moore Theater" was now complete and filed in the public record.

He'd known exactly what it would say from the day after it happened.

Jeremiah had been shocked when he saw the fountain of blood spilling from Alannah's casket, just as the audience had been. Some of them might have thought it was part of the act, but he knew better.

He had frozen into immobility, his mind flooded with the similar image of the blood when Suzette had been injured badly, twenty years earlier.

This time, though, it was Alannah. He heard her screams pierce the theater, and he knew she was going to die.

To top it all off, the lights went out. Alannah's screams stopped and he imagined hearing her last breath. Jeremiah collapsed on the stage, not wanting to believe he was responsible for killing the only woman he had ever loved.

He cried and couldn't move. At the time he had no idea how long he'd sat there in a heap. At some point the lights came back on and the curtain was lowered to hide him and the deathtrap from the audience. The giant circular buzz saw continued to spit blood. Somebody finally found the emergency button that caused it to lift up from the gory mess and stop.

He wanted to get up and save Alannah, but he knew that was impossible. He couldn't imagine seeing her remains.

Then somebody shouted, "She's gone!"

Gone?

What?

Several people crowded over by the box, and one of the stage hands lifted the two sections open.

"Oh, God . . ."

Jeremiah tried to listen. If Alannah was gone, maybe she'd somehow avoided death.

But "gone" could just mean "dead."

"So much blood," the stage hand said. He looked at Jeremiah and shook his head. "I'm sorry. There's no way she could have survived."

Having his hope crushed was bad enough, but then the police showed up. They started asking questions about the act. Even though he was clearly an emotional mess, they helped him to his dressing room and then asked more questions.

He finally found the courage to stand and walk step by step to the box.

Her body wasn't there. The only hint of the disaster was the flood of blood covering the stage.

After he explained to the police the basics of the trick, one cop, a tall, skinny, middle-aged guy with a pock-marked face and a grumpy attitude said, "We understand you had a problem with her. She had sex with one of the guys here and you witnessed it."

Jeremiah wanted to deny it, but somehow they knew. He just nodded.

"And you're known to have an explosive temper."

"I didn't kill her, if that's what you're asking. I loved her."

"Yeah. Sure."

The cop wrote some notes and then asked, "Where did her body go?"

"I don't know."

"Was there an escape hatch in that thing? Like a trap door?"

"No. Once she was in there, there's no way out."

"Seems there is."

"Somebody stole her when the lights went out."

"Who?"

Jeremiah snapped. "I don't know. Maybe you should fucking go look for them!"

He found himself standing threateningly in front of the cop, who stepped back a foot.

"Whoa, cowboy. Sit back down."

Jeremiah bit his lip to try to control his temper, and eventually he did find he could sit down.

"I didn't kill her, and I don't know where her body is."

The cop looked at his partner, who had just come back to the room. The partner was younger and a woman. She whispered to the other one.

They both came back to Jeremiah.

"You said there's no trap door."

Jeremiah nodded.

"But apparently there is."

"I designed the box myself and inspected it."

"Apparently not recently. The bottom opens. And there's are trap doors in the stage floor."

"Yes, I use those when I need to disappear."

"She must have let herself out of the box when the lights went out and headed to a hole in the floor."

Jeremiah stared at the cops as if they were speaking Greek.

"What are you talking about?"

"Would she know how to make fake blood?"

"Fake blood?"

"You ever use that in your show?"

He shook his head. "No, but she knows how to make it. I've told her before. It's not difficult. Corn syrup, chocolate syrup, and red food coloring will do it."

"Would you know it from the real thing?"

"Of course."

That's when they led him to the bloody box and he dipped his finger in gooey mess. He sniffed it and tentatively touched it with his tongue.

"I can't believe it," he said.

"Fake?" asked the woman cop.

"Yes!" he shouted. "It's fake!"

He could now see the newly created trap door inside the box as well.

"She's alive!" He shouted and smiled, not caring that his life had changed in the past hour more than he could possibly have imagined. All he cared about was that she was alive.

Somewhere.

* * *

The CSI report was 159 pages long. It took Jeremiah an hour to read the whole thing, and most of it was cover-your-ass bullshit. It detailed the process the investigators went through: who they talked to, the tests they performed, the follow-up calls they made, and, of course, how they came to their conclusions.

Once he stripped out all the crap, the actual factual information in the report consisted of only a few specific findings:

1. Alannah Clark had prepared fake blood and used it to make it appear that she was killed or badly injured as she was being cut in half.
2. She had encouraged an accomplice, Will Graves, an electrician and jack of all trades, to add a secret exit to the box.
3. Will Graves had also cut the lights for Alannah, allowing her time to escape the box, close the new exit, drop through the trap door in the stage, and leave the building.
4. Alannah might have been afraid of Jeremiah Moore due to her being indiscreet the day before.
5. Her current whereabouts are unknown.

Jeremiah closed the report on his tablet in disgust. It was such a waste of time.

Where are you, Alannah?

He closed his eyes. If only he could talk to her for five minutes. He would tell her how incredibly sorry he was that she felt so afraid of him that she had to escape.

Part of him wished he'd never told her that he had a history of having a bad temper. She'd never seen that in person, but she was so sensitive and fragile, he thought she must have built it up in her mind to be something incredibly frightful.

Maybe she was right, though.

He remembered his rage when he saw Alannah giving oral sex to that electrician. He'd avoided her for almost twenty-four hours after that, until the show began. They both had huge smiles on their faces for the audience, but inside, he was seething with anger. Her betrayal was all-encompassing, and he didn't know how he could ever forgive her.

She probably knew that.

Now, though, he knew, there must be more to the story. Over the past two years, he'd relived in his mind every minute they ever spent together.

Something wasn't adding up.

He had hoped the CSI report would help him understand why Alannah was the way she was, why she needed to run, and most importantly, where she was.

No answers were there, and now he needed to find them himself.

"It makes no sense that I still love you, but I do."

Saying it out loud didn't change things. He did still love her. He cherished her, wanted to be with her every minute of every day.

And he knew she felt the same way. She had to. No matter what he saw that day, he knew in his heart that was true.

* * *

Three months earlier, Jeremiah had tried to shake Alannah from his mind. The best way to do that, he decided, was to find another girl.

He went to a local bar and ordered a beer. As he sipped it right from the bottle, he tried to look friendly and open. It wasn't long before he saw a shy dark-haired woman glancing at him from the other end of the bar. She looked to be about thirty-five, much closer to his age than Alannah was. He almost chickened out but finally found the courage to go to her end of the bar.

"Mind if I join you?" he asked.

"Please."

She had a nice smile, and she was pretty by any standard.

"I'm Jeremiah."

"Amy."

And then he was tongue-tied. He didn't know what else to say. He looked at her and saw her bright eyes and the beautiful smile showing lots of white teeth. She had a full glass of white wine in front of her, so he couldn't order her another. He didn't know if he should ask about her background, her family, her love life, or her job.

It just felt wrong.

But now he was stuck.

"What do you do?" he finally asked.

"I work in an office. Computers."

"Oh, I see. I work at the dock. Nothing special."

She nodded and took a drink of her wine.

"I'm sorry, I just—"

He didn't finish, because he didn't know how. He just left a ten dollar bill under his beer and slunk out of the bar.

She'd been a pretty girl, nice, and there was only one thing that was wrong with her: she wasn't Alannah.

* * *

Jeremiah stood up and left the comfort of the oak tree. The sun was starting to set and it was a little chilly.

He liked St. Louis. It felt like home, but a home that had invisible bars holding him in. The only escape he had was the Internet, where he searched for Alannah Clark every day. His fingers flew through Google, the main newspapers, 411.com, and all the other web sites he could think of where he might eventually find her.

Every day, he hunted for the woman he loved.

One day, he knew he would find her again.

Chapter 22
2020

Savannah Clark woke, not sure where she was. Something was sticking into her side and she rolled onto her back. Sunshine filtered down onto her from between two buildings. She licked her lips and tried to remember what she'd been doing the night before.

Nothing came to her. She pulled herself up to a sitting position and glanced around. She was in an alley between two buildings. There was a dumpster between her and the entrance to the alley. It looked like she'd staggered there to find someplace to collapse.

"Shit," she mumbled.

She found her purse hidden behind the dumpster and was surprised to find her wallet, including credit cards and cash, intact.

"My lucky day."

She stood and took a deep breath while holding onto the brick wall. Traffic noises came from the street.

Farther down the alley two other people slept. Both men, and again she found herself surprised she was still in good condition.

She brushed her hair back and walked out of the alley. Almost immediately she recognized her downtown surroundings and headed over to the closest Starbucks.

The clerk was a young girl, maybe eighteen, perky, with a giant smile. "What can I get started for you today?"

Savannah knew the girl was staring at her wrinkled clothes. She wore a tight blouse with no bra and a tiny skirt. Clearly she hadn't been home to change. She pulled her coat tighter around her.

Fuck you, too.

"Just your dark. Whatever. Grande."

"Grande Ethiopian coming right up! Can I add something to eat to go with that?"

Savannah shook her head and scattered enough coins on the counter to pay for the coffee.

She took her drink to a seat by the window, trying to ignore everyone she imagined was looking at her. She didn't give a damn about them.

It was January 2. Four years to the day since Alannah had disappeared, and Savannah would mourn her lost sister any way she chose.

Part of her wished she smoked or took drugs. Anything to dull the pain of the horrible anniversary.

I miss you, Sis.

Over the past four years, Savannah had gained a lot of strength. She had been forced to rely on her own skills (such as they were) to survive. Alannah wasn't there to help make any decisions.

She thought she was doing pretty good. She had moved back to her hometown of Aynsville, New York, and she held down a job as a sales clerk at a local bookstore, had a small apartment that she was happy with, and was able to provide for herself.

She rarely dated, but she had one weakness. Sometimes, she found herself overwhelmed with guilt over everything that had happened. After all, Jeremiah had seen her with the electrician, not Alannah. That had led to the disaster of four years earlier and to her losing her sister.

So, who were strangers to judge her on the bad days? They didn't know the whole story, and she wasn't inclined to share it with anyone.

She sipped her coffee, and when it was finished, she walked back to her apartment and slept the rest of the day.

* * *

Jeremiah Moore was about as far away from Aynsville as it was possible to get and still be in the continental United States. He lived in the outskirts of San Diego, in a dilapidated three-story house. The owners rented him a room and made sure he knew that was all he was entitled to. He had to tip-toe to go down the stairs to the front door, so that he didn't disturb anybody else. There was to be no visitors, no cooking, no noise that could be heard from the floor below, and no bullshit.

That all suited Jeremiah fine, because the rent was half of any other place he'd seen when he came to town a year earlier.

Most of the people in the neighborhood seemed to be Mexican, and he was happy with that too. Less likely anybody would ever figure out who he was.

The one thing he did demand was access to the owners' Internet connection. He had a small laptop that he'd found in a second-hand store for $100. All it was good for was surfing the Net. He had no interest in game-playing or watching videos, so he didn't much care that it was as slow as a glacier.

Today he woke and realized it was four years since the disaster. Four years since he had lost Alannah.

As always, he felt that loss in his heart as deeply as he did on the day he'd ruined both their lives.

He'd long ago realized that everything that had happened was due to him misunderstanding things. Of course, *now* he knew he hadn't seen Alannah that day. It must have been her twin sister.

Alannah had told him she had a twin, and although he'd never met her, it seemed obvious now that that was who he'd seen.

It's the only thing that made the tiniest bit of sense. Alannah would never have betrayed him. Not in a million years. He hated himself for not seeing that earlier.

If he'd only realized that immediately. If he'd only talked to Alannah. If he'd only not terrified her into taking such an extreme action.

If only.

He had a small coffee maker in his room, the only thing he was allowed to use to "cook" anything. It only made two cups at a time, and the coffee was hot in a few minutes.

The laptop was ready for him when he sat down with his coffee. He signed in to his Gmail account and was surprised to see a Google Alert message.

After Jeremiah had lost Alannah, he set out on a desperate search to find her. Unfortunately, he soon ran out of ideas. It made him realize how little she had talked about her life before they met. He'd taken stock of what little he did know: She was born in a small town in New York state (but he didn't know which one); she had a twin sister (but he didn't know her name); her father was in prison for killing her mother; and that was it.

He had only a pathetic few clues to her background, but somehow he hoped he could use those bits to find her again. He'd set up Google Alerts to try to capture anything he could, but for four years, it seemed she had fallen off the grid completely.

Until now.

He tried not to get too excited. It might be nothing.

Clicking on the email alert, he found himself looking at a news story published a few days earlier.

LOCAL KILLER DENIED PAROLE

Brian James Clark, 60, formerly of Aynsville, was denied parole yesterday at Otalay Prison. Clark pleaded guilty twelve years ago for brutally murdering his wife, Marianne Clark (nee Burnside). He has never shown remorse for the murder and Judge Judith Mikerson called the proceeding a formality after testimony showed Clark had no regrets.

Nobody from Clark's family attended the proceeding. He is eligible for parole again in 2025.

Jeremiah read the story three times, trying not to get his hopes too high, but it seemed possible that this was Alannah's dad.

He checked and found that Otalay Prison was in New Jersey, about 100 miles from Aynsville.

Is that where you are, Alannah?

For once he felt real hope. The next clicks on his computer were to book a flight to New York.

* * *

The prison required approval for visitors considered as dangerous as Brian Clark. Jeremiah had to wait two weeks for the approval, and in that time he mostly sat in a motel on a little-traveled highway nearby.

Fortunately, nobody really cared if he saw Clark or not. He'd had no visitors other than his lawyer, and the approval slid through.

"Who the fuck are you?"

Clark looked more like eighty than sixty. His face was wrinkled and his eyes sunken, looking like beads glistening from a pillow of yellowish flesh.

Jeremiah tried to smile. "I'm a friend of your daughter."

"Daughter? What's that got to do with me? Haven't seen anyone in a decade. Couldn't give a rat's ass, neither."

"I read your trial transcript."

Clark stared at him and moved his mouth around as if trying to stop himself from drooling. Jeremiah wondered how he could ever manage to look after himself if he ever *was* paroled. He was pathetic.

There was a thick plane of glass between them, and they each spoke through a phone. Clark leaned back and shut his eyes.

Jeremiah continued. "I can understand why you killed your wife. She stepped out on you—"

"Did more than that. Treated me like a fool. It wasn't just once or twice, she did it like every week, out fucking some new guy and just giving me the shaft."

Jeremiah nodded, not believing a single word he was about to say. "I feel for you. We're not far from the same age and we could be friends if circumstances were different. Women just don't understand."

"What'd you say your name was?"

"Jeremiah. Jeremiah Moore."

"What'd you say you want?"

"I'm looking for your daughter. I hoped you could help me find her."

"What's she done now? Doesn't surprise me if she's got trouble."

Jeremiah was confused.

"Why's that? I thought Alannah would have been a model daughter to you."

"Alannah?" Clark stared at the glass pane and ran a finger down it, as if he was trying to judge its strength. "Who the hell is Alannah?"

Jeez, thought Jeremiah. *Is this guy an idiot?*

"One of your daughters. You have twin girls, right?"

"Don't know what you're smoking, boy, but I only had one girl. Savannah. No twins, no other girl, just her. An only child. Bad seed from the beginning, that one, caused enough trouble for two, but there is only the one of her."

Jeremiah stared at the old man, not understanding.

"You're sure?" He didn't know what else to say.

Brian Clark started to laugh, a long loud laugh, as he leaned back in his chair.

"Boy, I may have a few challenges with my life, but I think I'd know if I had a second daughter, don't you?"

"Do you know where Savannah is now?"

"Nope."

"You all grew up in Aynsville?"

"Yeah. Who knows, maybe she's there. I don't give a rat's ass where she is."

* * *

Aynsville was only a two-hour drive from the prison, but it seemed to take a million years to get there. Jeremiah had no clue what to think.

The town was bigger than he expected, about 20,000 people. He drove along the main street downtown, where there were a few dozen shops. It looked like the main street of any other town in America. There were the same people: the teenagers standing near a pizza joint, staring at him as he drove by; the old man with a walker, stopped to take a drag on his cigarette; the mom with three small kids trailing after her while she carried two bags of groceries home; the dozens of other forgettable faces that littered the landscape.

And then he saw Alannah.

She was walking in his direction, not paying much attention to anything. He had stopped for a red light and was waiting for it to change.

He saw her and his stomach lurched.

It's you, he wanted to cry, but no words left his mouth. He was frozen with shock at finally finding the woman he loved.

She looked exactly the same as he remembered her. Beautiful face, slim, and right then he knew once more that he loved her more than he could ever say. She was his life. Nothing else had mattered to him and nothing ever would.

I found you.

He rolled down the driver's window and stared at her long after the light turned green. Suddenly, the car behind him honked loudly and then magic happened: Alannah turned to see what the noise was all about and they locked eyes.

He smiled and started to call out to her, but she had a faster reaction than he did.

She covered her mouth with a hand and froze for a moment then turned and ran away.

Jeremiah was stunned at first but realized she probably still blamed him.

He gave the car some gas, but she'd turned around a corner. He got there and turned as fast as he could.

The ghost who was his soul mate was gone.

Chapter 23
2020

Savannah Clark was twenty-eight. Part of her felt that age, but part felt like she was a dozen or more years older. The past four years had been the worst of her life, probably the worst she'd ever go through.

She missed Alannah.

Every day she continued to write in the diary they had shared. Now, though, instead of writing to a mysterious and elusive *Diary*, she was writing to her lost sister.

"Dear Alannah" started every entry. She wrote about the everyday incidentals of her life, what she had for lunch, who she served at the bookstore, the weather. All this mundane stuff she wrote because Alannah could no longer experience any of it herself.

Less often, she wrote about her hopes and dreams for the future, because she rarely had any.

The saw that came down and ripped apart the coffin containing Alannah seemed to have truly buried her sister. She hadn't been seen nor heard from since that night.

Sometimes, rarely, Savannah would wake in the middle of the night and wander to the bathroom like a zombie, and she'd maybe feel a hint of Alannah in the air, as if she were a ghost who was trying to return.

Savannah would flash to become wide awake, and the sensation would disappear, along with her fantasy of being reunited.

The four years had trudged along like mud oozing down a hill after a rainstorm. Savannah spent most of her waking hours waiting until it was time to go back to sleep at night. Sweet, dreamless sleep was the only cure for her depression.

After that awful night, she'd wandered off in a daze. She had no more clue what had happened than anybody else. Once the theater was closed, she had found herself at the edge of the crowd leaving, and she just walked.

She barely stopped to pick up a few possessions from the apartment they shared, and then she walked again.

Three hours later, she thought it was safe enough to hitch a ride. When a fiftyish man picked her up and gave her the kind of smile she was used to, she climbed into the passenger seat, said she had a migraine, closed her eyes, and let him drive.

She ended up in Salt Lake City and stayed there for two years. The last thing she had wanted was to run into anybody she knew.

The Internet kept her up to date on the investigation, so she found out about the fake blood and that it seemed that Alannah might still be alive.

She didn't buy it. If Alannah was alive, she would know. She *knew* her twin was gone.

The wounds didn't heal in Utah, and eventually she woke up one morning and decided it was time to go home.

Not that she had any particular ties to Aynsville. Her mother was long dead, now her sister was no more, and her father was shuttered up in prison, as he deserved.

No family, but her origins were still there. She wanted the comfort of knowing the town she grew up in, and there was always a slim chance that going home would help bring herself back to life.

That didn't happen. Aynsville was familiar, but the depression stayed with her just as strongly as ever.

She thought the nightmare was behind her, though. Nobody would be looking for her in any case, but even if they were, she'd been gone from her hometown for a dozen years.

Then, as she was walking down the road, she heard that car horn and couldn't help glancing up.

Jeremiah Moore was there. Staring at her.

She froze, not knowing what to do.

Panic hit her.

She couldn't talk to him.

Why are you here? she wanted to scream. But, she knew.

He was there for her. For Alannah.

And he thought Savannah was her. She could see it in his eyes. Even though it'd been four years, she knew she looked the same as she had then, identical to her sister, and Jeremiah's face radiated with the love he'd shown her in the time leading up to that day.

She wanted to scream at him, to tell him to go to hell, to leave her alone and don't ever fucking bother her again.

Like that would happen.

He opened his mouth as if to call to her, but he was too far away.

Her head wanted to explode. She felt short of breath and her limbs tingled.

"Oh, God," she whispered. "Please just go."

But he didn't. He stared at her, and all of a sudden, she knew he was going to abandon his car in the middle of the intersection and run over to her.

Savannah didn't know what to do, but she had to get away. She ran and somehow kept running for an hour before she finally tripped and fell. She scraped her cheek and felt blood dripping from her forehead.

She cried. It wasn't from the pain, not from the memories, not from missing her sister, not even from seeing the man who caused Alannah's death. She cried because she had no other emotions left. She cried for the loss of her own identity, as she was stuck in the shell of a person who used to be fun-loving and alive.

She cried because she'd just as soon be dead as whatever she currently was.

Savannah wanted to go back and fix everything, but that wasn't possible.

She didn't recognize the neighborhood. Wherever she was, she hadn't been here before. She stood and walked back the direction she thought she'd come from. She was covered in sweat and probably looked half-dead.

Couldn't care less.

In the distance, she could see River City Church, whose spire was the tallest landmark in the little town. Once she saw that, she knew approximately where she was. She figured she was an hour from her apartment.

Halfway there, a hand grabbed her shoulder from behind.

She froze, knowing it was him.

"Alannah," said Jeremiah softly.

She didn't have the energy to run, and for that matter she didn't have the mental drive. She no longer cared.

Savannah turned to face him.

He looked the same, solid face, dark wavy hair, but he had aged, and not all that nicely. Four years had added two decades of wrinkles and droopiness to his face.

Guess we have something in common.

She thought about smiling, but that thought quickly passed.

"Oh, God, you hurt yourself."

He reached out tentatively, as if to rub the scrapes on her head, but he held back at the last second.

"You need a doctor."

"No, I'm fine."

He stared into her eyes, as if he didn't know what to say.

Finally he said, "You're just as beautiful as you were back then."

"I'm not her."

He blinked.

She took a step back. He'd been too close.

"I'm Savannah. Her twin sister."

He took a long breath.

"I talked to your father. I didn't understand, but he said there were no twins."

"Guy's a fucking idiot."

"He seemed—"

"He murdered my mother. He sat there waiting for the fucking cops to arrive."

She stared down at her feet and then lifted her eyes to face him.

"You know I'm not her. Jesus, man, you *know* it. And you know it was me giving that blow job. You fucked up big time, you freak. You killed my sister!"

"She's not dead."

"She is."

"It wasn't real blood."

"I know that! You think I'm fucking stupid or what?"

"I—I don't know what to think."

Jeremiah wiped his face with his hands. For a moment, it looked like he was going to cry.

Another thing we might have in common.

"Let me drive you home."

Savannah wanted to just leave him, but her body was aching and she didn't want to walk any more. She nodded and climbed into his rented Camry.

She gave directions to her place.

As they were driving, he said, "Where have you been?"

"Here. There. Around."

"I wish we'd had a chance to meet. Before."

She closed her eyes and wanted to sleep. A nice dreamless sleep.

"Sorry."

They got to her apartment and, without thinking, she said, "You can come up if you want to."

She instantly regretted it, not knowing why she'd invited him.

Maybe because he was her only tie to Alannah.

He nodded and she led him up.

"It's nothing special. Just a place."

When they got to the apartment, she told him to help himself in the kitchen while she cleaned up.

He got himself a glass of water and was sitting on her ratty old couch when she returned.

"It's uncanny how much you look alike."

Savannah smiled.

"I don't believe she's dead," he said.

She sat on a chair across from him.

"I don't think you realize how close we were. See the diaries over there?"

He looked where she pointed at a dozen books sitting on a shelf and nodded.

"We shared them. We were so close, we wrote in the same journal, as if we were two halves of the same person. We knew what the other person was feeling, what they had planned, and we were never far apart. We loved each other in a way you would never understand."

"I loved her, too."

She didn't answer.

He continued, "I still do. I will never believe she's dead. I will find her."

"I wish you could."

"What happened that night? Tell me what you know."

"I didn't know it was going to happen. She always told me everything, but not that time. All I knew was that she was terribly afraid of you."

Jeremiah's face turned sad, and he tried to smile to hide it but Savannah knew how he felt.

"Sorry," she said. "I didn't say that to hurt you."

She went to the kitchen and took a beer from the fridge. She held it up. "Want one?"

He shook his head. He joined her in the kitchen. "She knew I'd had a terrible temper in the past. And I knew how fragile a person she was. I hate myself for letting her think I could ever hurt her. I think I just felt so betrayed . . . ."

That's when he started to cry.

Savannah refused to comfort him, because she blamed him as much as he blamed himself. All she could manage was to push a box of tissue closer to him.

"Sorry," he mumbled between sobs.

She shrugged.

"She's still dead," she said.

Twenty minutes later, Jeremiah left the apartment and drove back to his hotel room. He felt more lost than ever.

But he still believed Alannah was alive.

Nothing would ever shake that feeling.

Chapter 24
2020

The little boy stood behind a tree and stared at his target.

The boy had died twenty-eight years earlier, and although he didn't know it'd been almost three decades, he remembered his death. The cold water carrying him away from his father, the quick glances of the canoe before it disappeared from sight, his dad calling to him before the voice evaporated completely and the rushing water carried him away.

He didn't remember the actual moment he died, not exactly, but he remembered swallowing a lot of water, choking and fighting, not being able to do anything to help himself.

He remembered that he eventually lost the fight and closed his eyes for the last time.

At least, that's what everyone had told him to expect when he died.

The old guy at the front of the church talked about going to heaven. That didn't happen, either.

Instead he found himself buried deep in the subconscious of another person. He'd lived there ever since, mostly sleeping.

He didn't like being dead.

At first he thought he might be in heaven after all. There was nothing to see or sense in any way, and he felt like he was sleeping most of the time.

Every once in a while, though, he could concentrate hard enough to catch a glimmer of where he was. The cold water that killed him was still weighing on him. He felt that cold water all the time, even though in some weird way he knew that was long behind him.

"I'm only ten years old . . . ."

It was that thought that sometimes came to him when he could find a bit of brain tissue that allowed him to think.

Only ten years old. Luke Harrison didn't miss his mom or his dad or his little brother, Dylan, although he sometimes found memories of them buried deep in his new brain. He remembered his Vavo, too, his mother's mom. She always made nice Portuguese meals and taught him how to speak the language. He didn't miss her, either. He wasn't sure why, but the only feelings he seemed capable of truly experiencing were hate and self-protection. More than anything else, Luke wanted to control the body he was carried around in.

That body belonged to a girl named Savannah Clarke. He knew little about her, because whenever she was in charge of the body, he was pushed down to the core stem, and he floated in a world of gray silence.

Sometimes, the other interloper took over the body. That was a girl named Alannah, but Luke hadn't shown up for the past four years. He had hoped she was dead so there was only one person he had to defeat to own the body, but he sensed that Alannah was starting to come back.

It was the older man's fault.

Alannah loved him.

Something had happened four years earlier to make her want to hide, but the man had come to find her, and her soul was rumbling in the rotten basement of the brain. She was awakening, and Luke couldn't allow that.

The imminent rising of Alannah had pushed Luke to take matters into his own hands, and this morning, he pushed hard enough.

For the first time, he controlled the body.

* * *

He snapped awake and took a long, deep gulp of air. It felt so good to swallow something that wasn't cold and liquid.

"I did it," he whispered.

Then he laughed. He stopped as soon as he started, because the laugh was nothing like any that had ever come from his own body. Then he laughed at *that*, since it shouldn't have surprised him.

He wasn't wobbly or weak when he stood. The autonomic nervous system took care of ensuring he could breathe, kept his heart beating, and maybe had something to do with remembering how the new body walked.

He felt hunger and thirst, feelings he hadn't experienced since he died.

Before sating himself, though, he was curious, so he walked to the bathroom and looked at himself in the mirror.

The girl who looked back had long blonde hair, and he knew that anyone would think she was very pretty . . . maybe even beautiful. Her face had no lines and when he smiled, she looked even more attractive.

He took off the T-shirt and shorts he'd been sleeping in and stared at the body. He'd never seen a girl naked before, and for a moment, he felt fear. He didn't know what to do.

Then, just as quickly, he remembered why he'd pushed so hard to take control of the body.

"I'm going to get rid of you, old man."

He took a drink of water and found an apple in the kitchen. He didn't know how to make much else to eat.

"Don't care."

He spent the next hour in the apartment. The biggest surprise was when he had to pee and found things different than he remembered.

Twice, he felt Savannah trying to take control, but he concentrated and pushed her back. He somehow knew that if he pushed hard enough, she would be forced into the same gray sleep he'd endured for so long.

But, it was very tiring. Both times, he needed to sit down and spend a few minutes recuperating.

"How do you keep me buried, Savannah?" he asked. Of course he received no answer.

The apartment was smaller than the house he remembered, and everything looked different. He couldn't figure out how to turn the television on for a long time, but then he finally found a small plastic device that let him turn it on and off.

"Where are you, you jerk?"

He knew the old man was in the same town. He was searching for Alannah, and that meeting must never happen. Alannah needed to stay dead and buried.

Unfortunately, he didn't know what the man looked like.

He searched the place but he couldn't find any photos. He did find the man's name—Jeremiah Moore—written in some diary entries, but there was no description other than to say he was eighteen years older than the twins.

Twins, my ass.

If anything, they were triplets.

His two sisters remembered nothing. They just knew the two of them had always shared the same body. Luke remembered, though. He remembered dying the same day that Savannah was born and, whether by fluke or design, found himself slicing through her consciousness, splitting it into two. Sometimes he imagined he was actually the father of Alannah, since his arrival created her. The three shared the body, but he was always the one with the least amount of control.

It wasn't fair.

He planned for all that to change. Starting right now.

He kept looking around the house, never finding a photo of his enemy. He did find something equally important, though.

"Oh, hello," he said as he pulled the revolver from its hiding place in a shoe box at the back of the bedroom closet.

The gun must have been placed there by Savannah. Goodie-Two-Shoes Alannah would never have had anything to do with it.

He laughed loudly, now more used to the girly sound of his voice.

Luke sat in a ratty old armchair, fondling the gun. Even at ten, he'd seen enough television to know how to use it, and his hands certainly had the strength to pull the trigger. It was perfect.

Then he realized how to find out what Jeremiah Moore looked like.

He closed his eyes and thought of Alannah. He chose her because she was weak, so deeply buried that he wouldn't accidentally give her control, which might happen if he started messing with Savannah.

The girl was deep. He searched his mind to find her, and for minutes, he couldn't feel her at all. He did run into a section of the core stem where Savannah was trapped, and he eased his way around her, searching for the other sister.

He was almost ready to give up ever finding her when he felt a tiny flash of a soul in the furthest recesses of the brain stem. He reached to her in his imagination and nuzzled up to her.

Alannah barely noticed he was there, and he took advantage of that. His mind sent out tendrils to her, massaging the sleeping girl, touching her, reading her feelings and thoughts.

He knew she was still buried in grief from the accident four years earlier. He thought she was being an idiot but kept that opinion to himself. He felt the gray depression draping her lost soul. Luke didn't allow himself to think about that. He didn't want to lose the strength he had through pity.

There was only one mission ahead.

He poked through Alannah's memories, searching for the one that would lead him to Jeremiah.

Finally, he found what he was looking for: a frozen image of Jeremiah as Alannah wanted to remember him. He was smiling and his eyes were full of life, full of love as he stared at his soul mate.

He knew that was how Alannah felt, and he barely suppressed a laugh.

Savannah, Alannah, and he were the real soul mates here.

* * *

Now he had the old man in his sights.

The gun was heavy but that was okay. His hand knew exactly how to hold it. Clearly, Savannah had done a lot of practicing with the revolver. He wondered briefly what plans she had had for it, but he figured she wasn't exactly a long-term-planning kind of girl, so she probably didn't have anything specific in mind. Just a feeling it would come in handy.

"You're right, sister."

Jeremiah was standing by a food truck. There were a half dozen of them in a row, and it took him a while to decide to go for the Thai food. As it was being prepared, he was looking at a cell phone.

Luke knew what the phone was by now. He'd learned a lot by studying the diaries that the girls had put together.

He was alone behind the tree, about thirty feet from Jeremiah.

No witnesses except the people in the food trucks, but they weren't looking. It was a cool day and there were no other people in the park that Luke could see.

He lifted the revolver and steadied his right wrist with his left.

Thanks for the training, Sav.

Slowly, very slowly, he pulled the trigger.

Even though his body knew most of the routine, he was still shocked by the recoil.

The gun shot was loud and scared Luke almost as much as the revolver pushing his arm backward.

He cried out in shock. The gun was on the ground, and he scrambled to pick it up.

He took one look back and was relieved to see Jeremiah lying on the ground, not moving, his chest covered in blood.

Chapter 25
2020

Alannah woke for the first time in four years.

To her, it felt like no time had passed, but subconsciously, she knew exactly what the situation was. Somehow, recently, she'd found a reason to want to come back.

Jeremiah was here.

Alannah was used to sharing the body with Savannah; they'd done that for their entire lives, and nothing particularly surprised to her. She never knew exactly what was going on when she wasn't in control, but she sometimes had a sense, like a long-lost memory that wasn't quite formed.

Jeremiah was back, and he had never meant her harm.

She knew that, although she wouldn't have been able to explain how she knew.

As was their longstanding tradition when they switched consciousness, Alannah first took stock of her whereabouts and then hunted for the diary.

The apartment was foreign to her, but reading the diary would bring her up to speed.

Back in Aynsville. That's a surprise.

It took her an hour to skim the diary. Four years of notes, four years of catching up. Once she was done, she went to the bathroom and was pleasantly surprised to see that her face hadn't changed. She didn't find any wrinkles or anything, just a slight lightening of her skin color.

She touched her cheek and it felt the same. Part of her wanted to laugh. Four years wasn't that long, but when you're only twenty-eight, four years was a seventh of your entire life.

If she looked closely, she could see the remains of a scrape on her cheek, but it was mostly healed. She never questioned minor things like that. Savannah's lifestyle was different from hers. "Jeremiah," she said to her reflection. "I need to find you."

Saying his name out loud brought back the overwhelming love she felt for him and a burning desire to find him. She needed to be sure he knew she wanted to be with him.

Always and forever.

She has no doubt he felt the same way. They were meant for each other, unlike any other couple she'd ever heard of.

Where are you?

That was the question she couldn't answer. Savannah's diary mentioned that he was in town, but that was several days ago, and she didn't know where he was staying.

She could wander the streets, but how successful could that be? Aynsville was small compared to Las Vegas, but it still had 20,000 people. Chances were slim to none that he'd be walking on the same street as she was.

Although it seems that's exactly what had happened a couple of days ago when he ran into Savannah.

She felt hunger pangs and wondered when the body had last eaten.

She closed her eyes and hunted through the images scattered among her short-term memories.

There was nothing about food, but she was shocked to find a shred of a memory of the body shooting a gun.

At Jeremiah.

That's what she thought it was, at least. She wasn't sure.

The image shocked her. She could tell it wasn't just imagination. The body was shooting at Jeremiah.

"Savannah? What?"

But, no, it wasn't her sister. She might have her quirks, and she was reckless, and Alannah sometimes thought she was out of control . . . but she'd never try to kill him.

Then she knew: it was the boy.

"Oh my God . . ."

Somehow he'd managed to take control of the body and had hunted Jeremiah.

She felt weak and leaned against the kitchen counter. The smell of rotting bananas was in the air.

Neither Alannah nor Savannah liked bananas.

She closed her eyes and concentrated. In the brain stem, she found Savannah, buried in a deep coma. She wasn't in a hurry to come back.

But the boy was. She felt the anger and urgency in his soul as he pushed to take the body back.

"No!"

Alannah had shouted aloud unnecessarily. The boy feel the force of her pushing him back.

She knew almost nothing about him, other than that he didn't belong. He had almost surfaced a handful of times over the years, but had never been strong enough to actually take control.

The anger floated up even more dangerously, and Alannah knew she had to be careful. Savannah and she needed to be sure never to let him be in charge again, ever.

She no longer felt hungry, but she did take a drink of water. It helped calm her.

The boy attacked Jeremiah, maybe killed him.

Alannah went to their computer and opened her browser, heading to the *Aynsville News* web site. It took her no time to find the story from four days ago.

> Yesterday at 4:10 p.m. Jeremiah Anthony Moore was shot in Alamo Park, near the Sunday food trucks. The assailant escaped and there are few clues. Moore was taken to Liberty Hospital with serious injuries. He is expected to live.

Freddie Barnard, who operates Freddie's Pizza, was nearby and told police the assailant was a woman. Another witness, Molly St. Clair, disputes that, saying the attacker was clearly a man, although thin with long hair.

Moore is not a resident of Aynsville. It appears he is visiting the town, but police are not commenting on his reasons for being here. They ask that anybody who has any information on the shooting to contact them as soon as possible.

"You're alive."

Alannah pursed her lips and touched Jeremiah's name on the monitor with one finger.

"I can't lose you again."

She read the online story a second time but there wasn't any information she didn't notice the first time. It didn't look like anyone would consider her a suspect, since there wasn't enough of a description to identify her.

Liberty Hospital was only a mile from her apartment. She remembered it from when she had lived in the town. In fact, that was where she and Savannah were born.

By the time she arrived at the hospital it was mid-morning. The sun was shining, making it a perfect autumn day. She wanted to keep that perfect feeling alive.

Alannah went to the reception desk and smiled at the middle-aged woman sitting there. The woman appeared tired as she frowned. It seemed to Alannah that she would always look that way.

"I'd like to see Jeremiah Moore, please. Can you tell me what room he's in?"

"Moore?"

"Yes. He was admitted here four days ago."

"I *know* who he is. Are you a relative?"

Alannah hesitated. "I'm . . . we're going to be married."

"You're engaged?"

"Yes."

The woman ("Christine" according to her name badge) stared at Alannah.

"How long have you been engaged?"

Alannah could imagine the nurse putting the word "engaged" in air quotes.

"Is that really important?"

"Just a minute."

Christine picked up a phone and dialed a number. She spoke too softly for Alannah to hear what she said.

"Wait there." The nurse pointed at a chair nearby.

Within two minutes, a police officer arrived. He was the opposite of Christine: young, bright, and attentive. His hand wasn't far from his gun, which made Alannah reconsider if this had been a good idea.

"Ma'am? You're here to see Jeremiah Moore?"

"Yes."

Alannah stood up and faced the cop.

"And you are his fiancée?"

"Yes."

"You may be the only person in the town that knows him. One witness indicated she thought a woman shot him."

"It wasn't me."

She knew she sounded defensive.

He turned to the nurse and lifted an eyebrow. She was just replacing the phone.

"He says he'd like to see her."

The officer asked her name and address. She was glad that he didn't ask for any identification. It'd be hard to explain why she said her name was Alannah when all her ID said Savannah.

Once he was satisfied he had what he needed, he walked her down a series of hallways to a private room. He opened the door and entered with her.

Jeremiah was in a wheelchair. Even so, he was smiling and leaning forward, as if he'd been hoping for a miracle and that miracle had just walked through the door.

"Alannah, it's you." His voice was soft, and that meant he was happy. She'd knew all his moods from the slightest change in his voice.

She ran to him, wanting to jump into his lap, but held back at the last second.

"It's okay," he said. "Hold me."

She did. She leaned in and put her arms around him, letting him decide how strongly to hug her. His chest was bandaged heavily.

"Oh, God. I can't tell you how happy I am to see you," she said.

"Me too."

He held her face in his hands and kissed her lips, tasting her.

They kissed and hugged and didn't have to say anything for several minutes. At some point, the police officer left the room.

Finally she sat in a chair beside him and held his hand.

"I met your sister."

"Yes, she told me."

"I'm glad. She looks like you, but the second you came in the door I knew it was you and not her. There's something about you. You've always been so quiet and gentle. I love that about you."

She smiled and squeezed his hand.

"I'm so sorry I left you."

"Where have you been?"

Alannah shook her head. "It's a long story, for another time. I'm just glad we found each other again."

He nodded.

She asked, "Do they have any leads on who shot you?"

"Not as far as I know. They don't really tell me much. I couldn't help, because I didn't see anything. I can only guess it was some crazy person."

"Probably."

"When can you leave the hospital?"

"I think it'll be on Sunday."

She nodded. "Three more days. I'll be looking forward to that."

She kissed him again and then just held him, loving the feel of his body touching hers.

* * *

Three days later, she was there. She'd actually been in his room almost non-stop since that first visit, only going home to sleep.

She didn't allow Savannah to have the body and certainly not the little boy. Savannah seemed to understand, not sending out any concerns. The boy was irritable, and Alannah kept having to push him back down. There was no way he could overpower her to take control while she was awake, and even when she slept, he was too immature to be able to do it. Most of the time, at least.

* * *

Jeremiah waited and when Alannah came to visit him on Sunday morning, he was as happy as he could ever remember. He was leaving with the girl he loved.

He could walk well, but he took it fairly slow on the advice of the doctors. They didn't want him ripping open his wound.

The bullet had scrambled his chest but somehow missed anything vital. His left lung had been grazed and some blood vessels were severed, which had led to a huge mess, but he was thankful that no serious damage was done.

The cops still had no clue who had shot him, and that bothered him. He'd heard rumors at the hospital.

"It was that girl, for sure," some said. "She matches what that witness said, and he doesn't even know anybody else around here. Who else could it have been?"

Jeremiah wanted to tell the whisperers to shut the fuck up, but . . . but, he didn't have a better alternative as to what happened.

He tried not to think about that.

As they drove to Alannah's place, she pointed out the schools she had attended and the people and other places that had some connection to her. He loved hearing every word. The town was much smaller than any place he'd ever lived, but he could imagine living here with her forever.

When they got to the apartment, Jeremiah was surprised to find that Alannah had planned an elaborate dinner consisting of sautéed scallops laid out on a bed of linguini cooked with mushrooms and a white wine sauce. It'd been a long time since he'd had such a nice meal, and he savored every bite.

Later, they ended up in bed together. Alannah was careful not to hurt him. She told him to lie on his back and she lowered herself onto him.

It felt so good to feel him enter her. It'd been so long, and at times he figured he'd never again be with a woman, since she was the only one he'd ever wanted.

They fell asleep in each other's arms, and his last thought was that he'd never been happier.

Chapter 26
2020

It was morning twilight the next day when Jeremiah awoke. He felt Alannah's hand stroking him and smiled. He was already hard and wanted to make love to her again, and it seemed she was just as interested.

"Shh . . . ," she whispered when she realized he was awake. "Just let me do this. Relax."

He nodded and closed his eyes again, enjoying the feel of her hand. He felt as aroused as the first time they had made love last night.

"I've missed you," she said. "I've thought about fucking you every day for the past four years."

He barely heard her. She was rubbing him harder.

"I'm close . . ."

"Don't you dare come without me!" She let go of him and leaned over to kiss him hard on the mouth. Her tongue slid inside and played with his. He reached over and felt her hard nipples, wanting to suck them but not wanting to break the kiss.

After a few moments, she moved to kiss his chest and he rubbed her hair.

"I love you," he said.

He could feel her nod as she moved down his body, kissing him all the way down until she took his shaft into her mouth and sucked. She pushed down as far as she could and let him feel the warmth of her mouth surround his cock. Her hands cupped his testicles, although he wasn't paying much attention to that.

He clenched the sheets, trying not to have an orgasm. It wasn't like her to be so aggressive, but he loved the change, and he remembered back to those few occasions years ago when she was more aggressive than normal.

"I want you inside me," she said.

Alannah climbed on top of Jeremiah and lowered herself onto him.

He could see her beautiful body and he loved it. He wanted to be with her forever.

She stared at him and smiled, a broad, captivating smile. He loved the way her hair bounced on her, how her cheeks were so lovely, and her eyes . . . well, they were more honed and sharper than normal, but that may have been the lighting.

Still . . .

She started to move up and down on him.

"I've missed fucking you. I forgot how good it felt," she said.

She groaned and bounced harder.

The night before, she'd been gentle, soft and slow, as she usually was. This morning, she was hard and looking out for herself. He could see in her eyes that she wanted only her own pleasure.

She pushed down hard and held him deep in her. He felt an amazing rush of pleasure as she somehow squeezed his cock over and over with her pussy.

He wanted to come. He needed to.

Jeremiah reached around her to reach for her ass and pushed her down even harder.

"Ooh . . . Squeeze my nipples."

He did as he was asked.

"Harder. Hurt me!"

Jeremiah was reluctant but squeezed her nipples harder. She groaned again and he increased the pressure.

She leaned back as she came, and that excited him even more.

"God, I love this!" she screamed.

It was the scream that was the last clue. Alannah just wouldn't do that.

He looked up at her and into her eyes.

"You're . . . you're not . . ."

She moved up and down on him again and laughed. "You love it!"

He couldn't help himself. He was coming and he grabbed at her body again, wanting to feel her all the way down.

Part of him wanted to stop, didn't want to betray Alannah, but his body wouldn't let him. He came, the longest orgasm he could remember, and it was pure pleasure.

But at the same time, he felt horrible. When he was spent, he relaxed and stared at the face looking down. She was still smiling.

"Thank you," she said. "I really did miss you."

"You're Savannah."

She just laughed again. "Took you a long time to figure that out, didn't it?"

He stared at the woman who was a twin to his soul mate. He still couldn't believe that he hadn't realized it wasn't her.

His cock had softened but was still inside the awful sister.

"How could you do that?" he finally asked. He moved her away from him and she stood beside the bed.

"Not a big deal."

She stood there, defying him to disagree. He just shook his head.

"Where is Alannah?"

"I'm going for a shower."

She turned and left the room and disappeared, slamming the bathroom door behind her. He heard her lock it.

Now that she was gone, Jeremiah felt a rush of guilt. How would he ever explain to Alannah that he had made love to her sister? Would she forgive him?

And how could he be sure it wouldn't happen again?

A stray idea crossed his mind: maybe it had happened before. She'd said she missed him. He pushed the thought away, not ready to deal with it.

The room was getting lighter as the sunrise brought life to another day.

Jeremiah found his clothes and dressed. He didn't know if he should wait around or leave, but he wanted to find Alannah. It was important that he talk to her before Savannah did.

The apartment was small and he heard the shower as he paced in the living area. There were two old armchairs and a damaged coffee table, probably second hand. A small TV perched on a bookcase. The armchairs were not positioned in that direction, making him wonder if they ever used the TV.

The bookcase was filled with notebooks, all identical in size. Most of them had black covers and a spiral spine, like notebooks a college student might use, but smaller.

He took one from the bookshelf and flipped it open.

It took him no time to realize these were journals or diaries shared by Alannah and Savannah. The entries mostly alternated.

What he also noticed immediately was that the handwriting of the two girls was identical.

That puzzled him.

He grabbed some other volumes at random, years earlier than the first one he looked at. Although the writing style had changed a little over a decade, the girls still wrote identically.

"How is that possible?"

Jeremiah put the books back and saw a smaller stack of books on the bottom shelf. They were heavy hardcovers with titles like *The DID Bible, How to Live With DID*, and *The Clinic Psychology of Dissociative Identity Disorder.*

He had no idea what the topic meant until he read the jacket of the first one.

> Once called a Split Personality and subsequently Multiple Personality Disorder, Dissociative Identify Disorder is one of the strangest and rarest of psychological situations.
>
> Two, three, or more individual personalities sharing the same body can be waved off as nonsense by those unfamiliar with the situation, but it's a real and very scary phenomenon.
>
> This book will help patients and their friends and families cope with this strange condition.

"What the hell?

He flipped through the book, but none of it felt real to him. How could one person have more than one personality? That was crazy.

The noise from the shower stopped and he put the book back.

Is it possible?

Savannah opened the bathroom door and walked to him. She was wearing a bathrobe loosely tied in front. Jeremiah could see most of her breasts and he found himself staring.

She laughed. "Like what you see?"

He blinked. "You're trying to tell me that you and Alannah are both here, right? Can she hear me?"

"No, she can't. It's like she's in a coma now. We refer to it as sleeping. We're both real in every way. She may have an empathic feeling for what is happening now but she gets no real information. That's why we have those." She pointed at the diaries. "So that we each know what the body has been up to while the other is in control."

"The body?"

She shrugged. "What would you call it?"

"I want to speak to Alannah."

"No."

"Why?"

Savannah walked over to the window and looked out.

"I'm not sure I want to hand over the body right now."

"I need to talk to her."

She shrugged. "I think you should go now."

"Why won't you let her talk to me?"

She shook her head.

Jeremiah felt frustrated and all of a sudden, a swell of anger overcame him. He recognized the feeling from the years when he couldn't control his temper, and he immediately felt like he wanted to just fucking hit the bitch and force her to let Alannah out.

He marched to her and grabbed her upper arm, turning her around.

"Hey! Let me go."

He shook her hard.

"Let me talk to Alannah. I need to talk to her, not to you."

"No!"

Without any conscious intent, Jeremiah found his hands on her neck, squeezing. His head felt like it was going to explode with rage. He knew what he was doing was wrong, but at the same time there was no way he could stop. His hands squeezed harder, and Savannah gasped and choked, trying in vain to push his hands away with her own.

Her eyes were wide and begging him to stop, but he only squeezed harder.

"Alannah, please come out," he said. "I'll stop if you come out."

Her voice was dull. "If she comes out now, she'll never share the body again."

Savannah tried to kick him but he was pushed against her and she couldn't gain any leverage. Her flailing was ineffectual and as he kept the pressure on, the fight left her and her arms dropped. Her eyelids started to close and—

Then she gasped with newborn energy.

The eyes were different. They were confused and scared, but Jeremiah saw the gentleness behind them.

He let go of her immediately and caught her before she fell to the floor.

Alannah choked and gasped for air. He helped her to sit on the couch.

"I'm so sorry," he said. "I lost control and thought that was the only way I could find you again."

She coughed. It took her several minutes before she could breathe easily again.

"What happened?" she asked.

He didn't know exactly how to answer. He was too ashamed to talk about how he'd made love with her twin earlier, even though that was really the start of what she needed to know.

"I saw the books. Your journals and the texts."

"Oh."

"Savannah wouldn't let you talk to me. I lost my temper with her and—well, you're here now. That's all that matters."

Jeremiah could see that she was a totally different person. The girl he loved was back. She was sweet and loving and shy, and he needed to protect her against everything. Even her own sister.

"She wouldn't let me out?"

"I don't understand it. She said something about how you might never let her come back."

"Oh."

Jeremiah hugged Alannah and then kissed her gently, the way she liked.

"It's okay," he said. "We're back together and we just have to make sure we stay that way."

She hugged him back and nuzzled close to him.

Chapter 27
2020

That night, after they made love again, Jeremiah held Alannah close to him in the dark and gently meshed his fingers through her hair.

"I think we need a key," he said.

"What do you mean?"

He nudged himself up onto an elbow so he could face her.

"I have to tell you something. It's not good."

Alannah was quiet for a moment and then said, "Do you still love me?"

"Always and forever."

"Nothing else matters."

Jeremiah wasn't sure how to tell her, but he finally just blurted it out.

"Sometimes, Savannah pretends to be you. I didn't know that until yesterday."

"She does?"

He nodded and took hold of her hand. "She's pretended to be you while making love."

"What?"

She sat up in the bed, shaking her head slowly back and forth.

"This morning. I'm so sorry. I had no idea it wasn't you."

"Oh my God . . ."

Alannah pulled her hand away from Jeremiah, but then she must have realized it wasn't his fault and she reached for him.

Silence hung in the air, and he didn't know if he should say more or not. He decided the best thing would be to wait for her to digest the news and decide what more she wanted to know.

"How many times?"

"I don't know. Once now. I think maybe a handful from when we were in Las Vegas."

"That bitch. She never said a word in the diaries."

"I know."

They were both quiet again. Jeremiah reached over to hug her and was grateful to feel her return the hug.

"We need a key. A phrase. Some way for me to be sure it's you and not her. If I hear you say it, I'll know it's you."

He felt her nod while pressing against him.

"What should it be?" she asked.

"Something you'll never forget. Something she would never say."

"I know it."

"That was fast!"

She pulled back and they looked into each other's eyes. There was a smile on her face, but it looked forced. He wondered how long it would take for that to go away.

"Our key is 'Always and forever.'"

He smiled.

They lay back down, and although it took a long time, they both eventually fell into a restless sleep.

* * *

Three hours later, the little boy took control of the body. He might only have a mind of a ten-year-old but he wasn't stupid. He could emote as well as the girls, and although he didn't have a clue as to exactly what was going on, he knew that Alannah had been in control and had been focused on some emotional issue.

Stupid girl.

It didn't matter what her problem was. All that mattered was that she was so busy concentrating on something that she had forgotten about him.

Normally when the twins slept, the last thought they had before drifting off was about the body.

If they were comfortable letting the other twin take control, they mentally handed the steering wheel over as they fell asleep. If they wanted to maintain control, *that* was their last thought, and their subconscious mind kept a lock on the cerebrum so that the other twin stayed in the dungeon of the brain stem.

Luke Harrison was trapped there too.

Even when one twin voluntarily gave up control, he had still been locked out, mostly. He didn't really understand why. Maybe because he was the intruder, and the brain didn't easily hand over control to an outsider? He didn't know and normally didn't care. When he was in the brain stem, his mind was sluggish, and he couldn't recognize the passage of time.

Tonight, though, Alannah had fallen asleep without locking the door.

Luke burst through, using every ounce of will power he could dredge up.

It worked. He blinked, looking out through the eyes of a twenty-eight-year-old girl. It was similar to how he'd taken control the week earlier.

Easier this time, he thought. He liked that.

Now Alannah was hibernating in the dungeon, along with Savannah, who had no idea of what was going on.

The old man is here. He wanted to chuckle, but he stopped just in time. *Don't want to wake him up.*

He smiled and carefully got out of bed. His eyes were adjusted to the darkness. The clock radio on the bedside table showed him it was 4:42 a.m.

He liked the strength of the body. Even though it was a woman, it was *way* stronger than the puny little body he'd died in. He could feel it with every step and every clench of his fist.

It still felt weird to have boobs, but he tried not to think of that. He was on a mission.

The kitchen. He found the switch that turned the light on in the oven. That cast enough of a glow that he could see shadowy outlines.

Luke pulled open the first drawer he saw. Pot holders and dish towels. He closed it again, trying not to make a sound.

There was another drawer on the other side of the sink and he shuffled to it.

Bingo.

There was a treasure trove of sharp knives, along with other silverware. He bent to get a close look in the low lighting and found the standard sets of knives, forks, and spoons, but beside the plastic silverware holder were two heavy-duty steak knives.

The body had long, blonde hair that was cascading over his face. He was annoyed at it and tried to shove it back, but it didn't stay.

Luke picked up one of the steak knives and read a small inscription: *Made in Portugal.*

The phrase reminded him of his Vavo, and he smiled. He had a passing thought, wondering if she was still alive or not. Not that he cared. Some of his previous life's memories might have clung to his soul, but none of the emotions.

He slid his finger over the knife edge. It wasn't terribly sharp, but that didn't matter for stabbing.

Luke knew that Alannah's phone could make a video recording and he thought he might take advantage of that, so that she could see how he had killed her lover. That would be funny. Unfortunately, he didn't know how to use the phone and this wasn't the time to figure it out.

Luke could hear deep sounds from the bedroom.

It's raining, it's pouring, the old man is snoring!

Hah!

Before he went to kill him, he stopped to be sure he really wanted to do it. He knew that there'd be a mess to clean up, and he'd likely have police trouble. He'd have to be a convincing liar.

"Actually, the girls can lie. They'll have no clue."

That made sense to him. If he let the girls take control afterward, they'd find the old guy dead and have to deal with it without knowing what happened. They'd be convincing and easily pass a lie detector test. He just couldn't be in charge of the body when that happened.

"Okay by me," he whispered.

He had to get rid of the old man. Otherwise, Alannah would keep control more and more, and he'd never have his chance to live again.

He deserved his time. He was still only a kid, and his own life had been taken too early. Here was the chance to fix that.

The old man was snoring louder. Luke went to the bedroom and stared at him. He was feeling nervous for the first time.

The man was sprawled on the bed with the covers tossed off of him. He wore only pajama bottoms with no top. He looked incredibly old.

Luke licked his lips. He could feel his heart racing and his breathing was faster.

His head was starting to ache.

One of the girls (or maybe both) was trying to stop him. He could feel the pressure building inside, as if he had the mother of all sinus colds.

"Screw you, bitch," he muttered.

He stopped dead, afraid his words might awaken the old man. He did stop snoring as loudly, but he didn't move.

Luke took a step closer and then another. He waited a moment and then found the courage to take the last two steps.

He was beside the bed, the old man close enough.

After taking a deep breath, Luke held the knife up above his head with both hands. He concentrated on the middle of the man's chest, imagining the knife flying down and being buried to the hilt.

He whispered, "Die, old man."

The man's eyes snapped open.

Luke was shocked, unable to move.

"Alannah?"

Disoriented from waking in the middle of the night, the man couldn't tell that Luke had a knife.

"Sweetie? What are you doing?"

Then he saw the knife.

"Oh, God."

The old man hesitated just a split second too long, as if undecided whether to put his hands up to stop the knife or to roll away. That split second woke Luke from his indecision.

He slammed the knife down with all his might, and, as he imagined, it sunk deep into his victim's chest.

The man flailed and screamed.

Blood spurted from the wound.

The old man tried to wriggle away, but Luke held the knife firmly and twisted it, releasing a bigger flood of dark blood.

The man tried to lift his arms but couldn't.

He stared up at the woman he loved in complete confusion as he died.

Luke held onto the knife for a few minutes that seemed like forever. When he was sure the old man was dead, he laughed.

Chapter 28
2020

Alannah woke up, wondering how long it'd been since she'd had control of the body. It seemed like a long time.

She was in the bed she'd shared with Jeremiah, and she smiled as she thought of them making love. That was her last memory before falling asleep.

A faca esta afinada.

"What?"

The weird phrase lingered in her mind, but she had no idea what it meant. Whatever it was, an ominous chill ran through her.

The little boy was out.

"Oh my God, what happened?"

She stood and looked around the room. At first she didn't see anything unusual. The blanket on the bed was messed up, but that could have just been from Jeremiah getting up. She glanced at the clock: 7:34.

It happened at 4:42.

She wasn't sure what "it" was, but the phrase rose from the brain stem, covered in gray.

Then she saw the speckles of blood on the sheet. Not much, but enough. She stared at the dots, knowing that there had to be more blood somewhere.

She shuffled around the bed slowly, not really wanting to find what she already knew was there.

When she saw Jeremiah's body on the floor, she froze. She wanted so much for this to be a dream, but it didn't feel like one. The colors were too bright, the splotches too detailed, the grimace on his face all too real.

She didn't scream and didn't faint, although she was close to doing both. All she did was stare.

His body was ripped to pieces, surrounded by the blood that had flowed out of his chest.

"I need you," she said. Even as the words left her mouth, she knew it was stupid. He couldn't be there for her ever again.

She thought she could hear laughter in the brain stem, but that was impossible. *He* wouldn't know what was going on and certainly couldn't react to it.

"You fucking asshole," she whispered. It was the first time she'd ever said either word.

"Jeremiah, I'm so very sorry."

Finally, she collapsed onto the floor beside him, crawling close to him. She closed her eyes and slipped her arm under his neck crying into his shoulder. She hugged him, not noticing how cold he was. She wanted him to hold her and tell her he loved her.

Her whole life, she'd never had anyone cherish her like he did.

"Don't leave me alone."

She rubbed her hand on his face, feeling him one last time.

Alannah remembered the first time they'd met, outside the dance studio. She remembered how he watched her dance and how it made her feel special.

She remembered their first dates and the first time they made love. She remembered all the times he took care of her and made sure he cradled her insecurities and shyness. Somehow, she knew that she only had that portion of a full personality and that Savannah ended up with the courage and outgoing parts, but Jeremiah had always treated her with the tender care she needed.

There would never be anybody like him.

"I love you," she said. "Always and forever."

She wiped some tears away.

"You wanted a key to know it was me, and I never got to use that key. He got to you instead."

She rose on one elbow and closed his eyes. Then she gently kissed him on the lips, saying one last silent good-bye to him.

* * *

She left his body twenty minutes later, taking the blood-covered knife with her. She went to the kitchen and rinsed it off. She needed to scrub the blade to clean off the congealed blood.

It never crossed her mind that the police would blame her. They were already suspicious of her from when the little boy had shot Jeremiah earlier. When they found out he'd been killed after sleeping in the same bed as hers, and when they found her fingerprints all over the place, well, it wouldn't take a big city CSI team to figure out she was the killer.

Even if she wasn't.

But none of that mattered to her. She wasn't thinking about the police, or anything else for that matter. Her brain seemed sluggish, and she was only following what instinct told her to do.

She dried the blade and walked back to the bedroom.

Her pajamas were covered with blood. She didn't care about that, either.

She lay down beside Jeremiah's body and arranged his arm beneath her neck. They needed one last cuddle. Her leg touched his, and she thought of the times she'd woken up in his arms.

Alannah held the knife in both hands, above her chest. She closed her eyes and thought of being with Jeremiah again.

Chaos erupted in the brain stem, but she pushed her other selves—*both* of them—deeper, ignoring their protests. Neither Savannah nor the little boy wanted to die.

Too bad.

She concentrated on the knife, knowing she needed to do this, and knowing also that it would be the hardest thing in her life.

"I love you, Alannah."

She hesitated, almost sure she heard Jeremiah's voice. She blinked her eyes open but the body beside her was still lifeless.

Just wishful thinking.

"Always and forever."

Still not real.

She took a long, deep breath and pulled the knife down as hard as she could, slamming it into her own chest.

She screamed. All three of her personalities screamed for her to pull the knife back out, but she fought the urge and pushed it harder into her chest.

The pain was worse than she imagined, and she couldn't breathe. She wanted to stop, but she pushed one last time, barely nudging the blade.

She cried, but her mouth no longer made any noise.

Her last thought was no surprise.

"Always and forever."

Epilogue

The little boy floated again in the misty abyss. He had been yanked from his body and now was flying through a gray emptiness.

"A agua esta fria."

The water is cold.

He remembered that. He remembered he once had a father and a mother, and he'd fallen into the cold water from a canoe.

He remembered an older woman, his vavo. She spoke funny words and although he understood her, he no longer remembered her face. Nor did he miss her or his parents. The concept of missing somebody wasn't really there anymore.

"A faca esta afinada."

The knife is sharp.

The second death was different. His body-sister had killed, but he only vaguely remembered that, too. And he didn't care.

Nothing mattered except floating in the gray mist.

Then he slammed down into a mushy landing. He had no sense of time, and this new brain wasn't expecting him.

Somewhere he heard a baby cry.

"Hello, little brother," Luke said.

John R. Little published his first short story in 1982 and hasn't stopped since. He's published fifteen books so far and has many more ideas finding find their way to print. John won the Bram Stoker award for *Miranda* in 2009 and was nominated three other times (*The Memory Tree*, *Ursa Major*, and *Little by Little*).

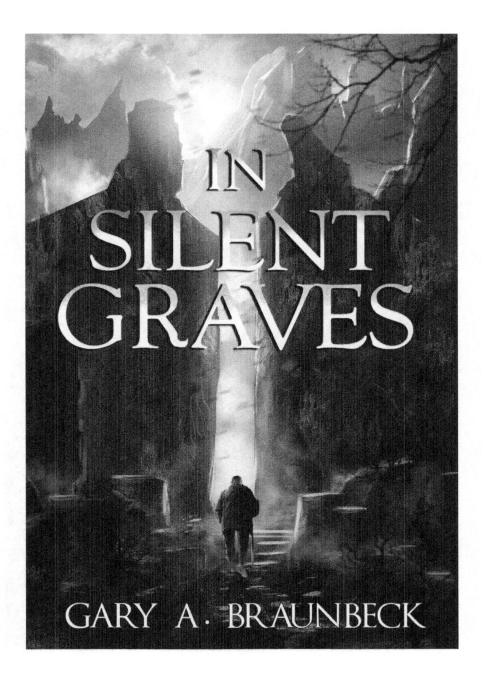

IN
SILENT
GRAVES

GARY A. BRAUNBECK

DAVID LISS
PALEO

JOURNALSTONE'S DOUBLEDOWN SERIES, BOOK VI